GW00836421

TALES OF A YOUNG RIDER

Happy Trails!
Patrice Engle Spyrka

PATRICE ENGLE SPYRKA

ILLUSTRATED BY ANDRAYA SPYRKA

ISBN 978-1-0980-5617-9 (paperback)
ISBN 978-1-0980-5618-6 (hardcover)
ISBN 978-1-0980-5619-3 (digital)

Christian Faith Publishing, Inc.
832 Park Avenue
Meadville, PA 16335
www.christianfaithpublishing.com

Printed in the United States of America

To the YMCA of the Rockies, Snow Mountain Ranch.
To Rudy and Clara Belle Just, who taught me so much.
To my sister, who joined me on many adventures.
To my family, who provided an amazing place to grow up in.
And to all the horses that have enriched my life.

CONTENTS

PREFACE

Growing up at the YMCA of the Rockies, Snow Mountain Ranch, was truly a magical experience. I moved to SMR when I was four and had my first horse when I was five. There were so many things to do that it was impossible to be bored. Even as a child, I never took the beauty of the ranch for granted. God's creation could be seen everywhere, and it was a spiritual experience for me every day.

We kept our horses at the Just Ranch and visited with the Justs frequently. They were true pioneers living the pioneer life. Always concerned for the animals and the land, their existence had a different meaning and priority. We would sit for hours and listen to them bring history alive. They were gentle and loving people. Their wealth of knowledge was built from the experiences gained through their heritage. They both were excellent horsemen who enjoyed gardening, ranching, animals, and nature. Clara Belle loved her Native American culture: hunting and tanning like she was taught. She was a crack shot with a rifle and received her first gun from an outlaw horse thief. Rudy spent four years in the armed services enlisting at the beginning of World War II, bringing home three bronze stars—a distinguished unit badge and a good conduct medal. He never stopped learning or appreciating what surrounded him. They both remind us that our heritage should not be forgotten.

My parents met at YMCA of the Rockies, Estes Park Center, in the 1950s. My dad was a wrangler, and my mom worked in housekeeping. They both loved the Colorado mountains and horses. After finishing his master's degree in *Y* work and eight years in management, he accepted the position of managing director of Snow Mountain Ranch where he remained for fifteen years. The rich experiences I grew up with have left a stamp on my heart, and I am so happy to share them.

Patrice Engle Spyrka
TalesofaYoungRider.com

CHAPTER 1

THE JUST RANCH

The tops of the pine trees could be seen through her bedroom window as they stood against the bluebird sky.

"What a beautiful Colorado morning!" Leah sprang out of bed and pet her dog between the ears. Nicki yawned while her tail curled up behind her. "June is my favorite month of year. The grass is green, the sky is blue, and the mountaintops are still white with snow." She grabbed her jeans and Western shirt off the saddle rack in the corner of the room, then pulled her boots on and headed out the door.

"Wait for breakfast!" her mom yelled as she pushed the screen door open. Leah stopped, backed up a few steps, and turned to the kitchen to grab a warm muffin.

"Thanks, Mom!" She smelled the muffin. "Oatmeal muffins, my favorite."

"Which horse are you riding today?" Mom asked. "And where are you headed?"

"I'm not sure yet," she said, muffled by the muffin in her mouth.

There were many different rides to go on: some had creeks, some had trees, some had steep hills, some had meadows, and some went over mountains, but all were within the 5,200-acre ranch Leah's dad managed as the director of YMCA of the Rockies, Snow Mountain Ranch. Her mom worried the entire time she was gone.

"Be careful today. I am hesitant to let you go without your sister. The rivers are running high from the spring thaw and the hungry bears are coming out of hibernation. Tell Rudy which way you head," Leah's mom reminded her.

"I will, Mom. I'm twelve years old, you know. And no, I don't need Kacy to go with me." *Slam*, the screen door went as she ran down the stairs of the "Yankee Doodle" cabin.

The walk to the Just Ranch was welcomed as Leah warmed up in the brisk morning. She loved living in the mountains of Colorado. At nine thousand feet above sea level, it was a magical land. Lodgepole pine trees carpeted the hills and mountains. White aspen trees with dainty green leaves were sprinkled throughout the landscape. Rugged mountains rose up out of the valley floor. The air was crisp and clean at that elevation, and all the colors of the sky, grass, and flowers were especially radiant.

The ranch where her horses were kept was a mile from her house down a dirt road that had ups and downs like a rollercoaster. South of the Admin Building was a small pond. Silver sage and Aspenbrook lodges were on the right, then the old firehouse on the left. Rudy's ranch panel gate was the last hurdle, and then beautiful old growth pine trees could be seen. She could walk, run, or bike to the ranch, but rarely did she get a car ride down.

The Just Ranch was a wonderful place within the Pole Creek Valley. It was full of animal friends, delightful sights, and the most interesting "grandparents." They weren't really her grandparents, as she wished. Rudy and Clara Belle Just were ranchers who were filled with wisdom from the nature and animals that surrounded them. Visiting the Just Ranch was like stepping back in time.

Cluck, cluck, cluck, cock-a-doodle-doo, clucked the chickens as Leah walked up the final hill. The log chicken coop sat at the entrance to the ranch and had wide, brown logs that were chinked with a manure mixture for insulation. The west end of the coop had a sloped, rusty tin roof with bins for coal and firewood underneath it. Chickens could be seen roosting from the upper windows. The rest of the chickens were out in the yard, pecking the ground, slowly walking with their dinosaur legs.

Rabbits hopped throughout the barn yard in a sort of rabbit heaven. All colors could be seen: black, white, tan, brown, gray, white with gray patches, white with tan patches, white with brown patches, and black with white spots. They hopped around sniffing the ground, looking for food. They stopped. Their noses twitched and whiskers moved. Their ears pricked up as they searched for signs of danger. Some burrowed into the ground and made a nice soft bed to lie in.

The goats spotted Leah and ran over to see her. Oliver was brown with two big white patches on either side of his stomach and splotches of white on his legs. Elvis was black with a white tail and patches over his ears. Leah kneeled down and played with them.

"Hey, Oliver, you can't eat my hair!" She pulled her long blonde hair out of his mouth. He jumped on her back. Elvis grabbed her finger and chewed it like it was a carrot. Leah held his muzzle in her hand. It was so small and soft. His teeth were lined up on the bottom of his mouth and he had a soft pad at the top of his mouth. She kissed him on the nose, and then he bounced back to his mama. Oliver sprang off her back and followed him, bucking along the way.

The old log machine shop across from the chicken coop looked like a museum. Antique tools and tractor parts filled two small rooms with a breezeway in between. Cables hung from railroad spikes that were pounded in the wood. Next to the tools hung a frame displaying a faint handwritten poem on yellowed paper titled "Old Things." She struggled to make out the words.

"Hey there," a cheerful voice said from behind the rusty tractor that stood in front of the breezeway.

"Hi, Rudy!" Leah jumped and popped out of the small room. "What are you working on?" There were strips of wood that were wrapped in plastic and looked like long triangles.

"I am making covers for my strawberries. It gets too cold at night for them to thrive. This way, the day's warmth will be trapped next to the plants and they will be protected from the morning cold." Rudy hammered the last nail in and neatly stacked the remaining wood. All of the ranch tools were stored in the shop, huge chains hung from the ceiling, and different-sized hammers and chisels lined the workbench.

"Why do you have so many tools, Rudy?" Leah asked, noticing the layers of dust and cobwebs that covered them.

"Well, now, most of the tools hanging here were used by my parents, Karl and Della Just. Long ago, the ranch was just trees, rocks, and sagebrush, and now it is lush hay meadows and ranch buildings. This ranch was sculpted out of the rugged land and harsh elements," Rudy said, putting his hammer away.

"You know," he said, "my daddy made the voyage on a ship across the Atlantic Ocean from Vienna, Austria, to America in the late eighteen-hundreds, while my mama traveled over the mountains in a covered wagon when she was just two years old." He paused for a moment as if reliving the journey, then pointed to the mountains at the end of the valley. "They struggled to cross the wild, untamed country to get to the West. The railroad over Rollins Pass wasn't built yet, so their teams of oxen, horses, and canvas-covered wagons traveled over the steep, unforgiving mountains on a route called Middle Park Wagon Road."

Rudy ran his hand down a pair of old rusty pliers. "In fact, this small room was the original building on the ranch. In 1893, my grandfather paid fifty dollars for this little cabin and the squatter's rights, and that is how the Just Ranch got started. The 320 acres grew to nearly three thousand acres that is now part of the YMCA."

Rudy leaned on a shovel for a minute, then quietly bent down and picked up a rabbit that had come into the shop.

"There, now," he said as he stroked the rabbit behind the ears while cradling him in his arms. The rabbit was white with several brown spots scattered throughout its body and had solid brown ears. He enjoyed the scratch, and then hopped down to look for some fresh grass.

"We will sheer sheep later today." Rudy handed Leah a square-bottom shovel. "Would you like to do some chores with me first?"

"Sure, I would!"

There were many chores to do: cleaning barns, mending fences, repairing equipment, feeding stock, collecting eggs, and tending to the garden, to name a few.

"Let's start by cleaning out the stream." Rudy walked over to the small stream. It was used to water the chickens, rabbits, guinea hens, and pigeons. The slow, trickling water meandered in between the shop and the chicken coop, then cut across the path just before the round grain bin.

"Scrape out the excess dirt and rocks so that the water can flow more smoothly," he said, pushing his black square glasses up. "Throughout the day, the chickens drink and clean themselves in the water and dam it up."

Rudy wore a red flannel shirt, jeans, rubber boots, and a work hat that covered most of his white hair. His hands were big and strong, and his body was used to the demands of ranch work, making it look easy. Leah tried to keep up with Rudy, but the shovel was too heavy. She ended up making the stream wider and water raced down the new channels she created.

"Baa, baa, baaaaa."

Leah looked up in time to see Clara Belle walking up the hill carrying a bucket with a lamb frantically running after her.

"Hi, Clara Belle, who is your friend?" she asked.

"This is Lammie," Clara Belle said lovingly. "He was born with a clubfoot and abandoned by his mother." Leah looked down the leg of the young black Hampshire lamb. There at the bottom of his left front leg was a leather strap with a pad tied onto it.

"I made him a boot so he could walk." Rudy rubbed his head and grabbed the bottle from the bucket. "He is expecting breakfast. Would you like to feed him?"

Leah took the old glass Coke bottle and held it out for Lammie. He grabbed it and drank it as fast as he could. He made sucking noises as his tongue gripped the nipple. His front legs were wide, and his stomach grew bigger and bigger. When he finished, he had white foam around his muzzle. Leah put the bottle back in the bucket and handed it to Clara Belle.

Clara Belle was part Cherokee Indian and the best ranch hand around. Cowboys from long ago admired her abilities as a cowgirl, for "she could shoot a gun better than any of 'em," Rudy would say proudly. Clara Belle dismissed his praise as simply being her job. She was short, round, and had brown hair that hung down from her skunk hat. She had tanned the hide of a dead skunk she found on the side of a road and made it into a hat. The tail on the back made her look like Davy Crocket. There wasn't much she couldn't do, including tend to the animals, recite poems, ride horses, grow beautiful flowers, cook the best bread and pies, and tan leather into soft garments.

Rudy smiled at Clara Belle and asked, "Whatcha got there?"

Clara Belle pulled a long strip of purple ribbon from around her neck. She winked at Rudy. "Come here, honey," she said to Leah. "Let me fix you up."

Leah sat down on the concrete foundation of the grain bin next to Clara Belle. "I'm going to braid this ribbon into your hair so you can feel like a real Cherokee Indian. Today is a busy day with sheep shearing and you don't want your hair to get into the way."

She parted Leah's hair and braided the purple ribbon into the braid. Next, she pulled it across her part in the back and braided the ribbon down into the other side.

Charlie came over to see what was happening. The white goat was a pet that had been on the ranch for years. He was lent out to a dude ranch in Winter Park for most of the year. He let out a muffled bleat, and then positioned his head in Leah's lap for a scratch.

"There, now. How does that feel?" She finished the braid and grinned at Leah.

Leah leaned down to admire her reflection in the stream. The purple ribbon was braided throughout and hung down from the ends of her hair. She stood up and gave Clara Belle a hug.

"I love it! Thank you, Clara Belle."

Rudy grabbed the shovels and opened the door to the grain bin. The cylinder grain bin held fifty-pound sacks of feed for the animals. Leah hopped up and followed him into the tin building where he began tidying up. Large oak barrels lined the edge of the bin and were filled with lamb's feed, racehorse oats, and alfalfa pellets or "horse cookies." The racehorse oats were her favorite. She buried her hands in the wholegrain, then pulled them out and let the kernels fall through her fingers. Next to the oat barrel were her bridle, mud boots, and the cookies she needed to catch the horses.

"Grab yourself a bucket," Rudy said, pointing to several buckets stacked on top of each other. "Let's go feed the lambs." Leah grabbed a tin bucket and Rudy filled it three quarters full with lamb's feed. He handed it back to her. She grabbed it, and it immediately fell to the ground. Her arms quivered with the weight so she had to take small steps to the trough. Rudy filled a bucket for himself and headed out toward the sheep corral.

"Pour the feed out into the trough and make sure you fill the entire length, so all the lambs get a chance at it." Leah carefully poured the feed out into long wooden troughs, and as she did, the bucket slowly got lighter. The lambs pushed their way in, almost knocking her over as they munched on the feed. Once empty, Rudy took Leah's bucket from her and stacked them together. He stopped by the horse barn, which stood next to the grain bin.

A swinging half door to the horse barn displayed two aluminum racehorse shoes on the top rail. As Leah approached the doorway, frantic pigeons flew out of the barn. The *flap! whoosh!* from their wings startled her and made her duck out of the way. Inside the barn were two large stalls and three smaller ones. Large harnesses were draped over wood posts that came out from the barn wall. Rudy reached up and hung a spare throatlatch from a bridle that he had found in the grain bin.

"Why do you have these harnesses?" Leah asked. "You don't have any draft horses."

"These harnesses haven't been used for years but tell a story of the kind of work that used to be done on the ranch," Rudy said, wiping bits of straw and pigeon droppings off the leather. "Teams of horses did all of the work that tractors do now. They moved logs, cut hay, cultivated fields, and even plowed snow." Rudy pointed to a piece of harness on the far post. "At one time, we had about two dozen head of horses, including teams of draft horses, ranch horses, and a few colts. Do you see this bridle here?"

Leah looked through the dim light to see the harness bridle. Over the square blinder, which partially covered the horse's eye, was a round bronze medallion with "U.S." stamped in it.

"This harness had once belonged to the U.S. Calvary," Rudy said proudly.

In the back corner of the barn was a ladder that led up to the hayloft. Some of the summer's sweet, loose hay was stored there. Leah climbed up the ladder while Rudy cleaned the stalls below. Carefully and slowly, she tested each board before putting her full weight on it. There were many holes in the floor of the loft, and she didn't want to fall through. Once she knew the floor was solid underneath her, she leapt up and down in the fresh hay. *Yahoo!* She squealed and jumped and tumbled. In a few minutes, she was tired and lay down. Using the soft hay as a blanket, she covered herself from head to toe.

The ends of the barn were open so the hay could get plenty of ventilation and not get dusty, moldy, or wet. If the hay got wet or was not dried in the field properly, it could get "hot" and actually catch fire just like it did at the Littlejohn's place. The hay was put up, and two weeks later, it burst into flames. Joe Littlejohn lost his entire barn. But Rudy's hay was as fresh-smelling as the day he put it up. She dozed there for a minute.

Outside, the ewes and lambs began bleating loudly. Leah sat up and looked through the space in the log where some chinking had fallen out. The two sheep barns were beside the horse barn and had small square doors and small stalls inside. Some of the ewes were inside the barn, the rest were in the corrals. The corrals were made of logs tightly stacked on top of each other so hungry coyotes couldn't get in. The gates were tall and made of smaller poles. The other sheep barn stood in the flat part of the valley. It was not used much, unless the sheep wanted to get in out of the rain.

Leah looked down the valley as far as she could. It had lush meadows with the best, most nutritious mountain grass. Pole Creek divided the meadows and willows followed the creek's path. Several mountains along the western slope of the divide were visible from the Just Ranch. On the left side of the valley were the jagged Indian Peaks. Devil's Thumb protruded out of a saddle near the Indian Peaks. Close up, it was just a pile of rocks, but down in the valley, it was a well-known landmark that could be seen for miles. To the right of Devil's Thumb, were James Peak, Bancroft Peak, and Parry Peak. Snow Mountain was directly next to the ranch, which old timers knew as Sheep Mountain. The mountains commanded the landscape in the valley below.

"Hello, friends!" Leah greeted the mountains.

Outside the barn, Rudy and the ranch hand broke her thought. They were working in front of the sheep barn and discussing the shearing procedure. Dust rose from the corral as the sheep walked within it. Some had collars with bells that rang out when they moved. They helped Rudy know where they were and when they were in danger. The sheep *baa'd* loudly.

Leah jumped out of her pile of hay, picked the last of it out of her hair, and scrambled down the ladder. Clara Belle herded a dozen sheep into the pen, then grabbed the first ewe, stroking her and speaking softly to calm her.

"Torrance, grab that ewe from Clara Belle and we'll shear her first," Rudy said, as he prepared the clippers. Torrance hugged the sheep behind the front legs and tipped her back. She sat on her rump with her four legs off the ground. Rudy grabbed the ewe and placed her between his legs, then ran the clippers up and down her belly and legs. It was like a precision dance of Rudy moving around the sheep, allowing different pressure points to expose a smooth path for the clippers to run on. The ewe popped up and Rudy finished the job shearing her back. The entire process took just minutes. It didn't hurt the sheep, but when Torrance let her go, she protested with a long "BAAAA" and headed back to the others.

In the place of the ewe was a pile of soft wool. Clara Belle gathered it up in her arms and threw it into the large burlap wool bag that hung from a rusty hoop mounted on the top log of the corral. Before more went into the bag, she tied "ears" on the bottom of the bag for easier handling. The bag was seven and a half feet tall and fit about thirty-five fleeces. Rudy turned to shear the next one Torrance had ready. He worked feverishly to get each sheep sheared in minutes and with each sheep that was sheared, the large burlap bag filled up more and more with wool.

"Leah, climb up in there and be my stomper." Rudy pointed to the bag. "That way we can pack the wool down and fit more into it."

Glad to help, she climbed up the log fence and scooted across the top rail until she was over the wool. The bag was almost full, but when she jumped into it, she sunk down and it tickled her tummy.

"Stamp it down with your feet so it gets nice and compact," Rudy said. Leah marched her feet up and down to press the wool and make more room. By the time the next sheep was done, she had to pull herself out of the bag to let Clara Belle add more in. She kept working the wool until it was only about two inches from the top. The bag was bursting at the seams. Rudy climbed the log fence to lift the burlap off the ring. Torrance held it upright until Rudy closed it with twine, using a sling stitch. It was so heavy that it took two of them to carry. They put it in the horse barn so it would be kept safe until Rudy took it to market. Eventually, the wool would be sold to make sweaters and blankets.

"That's enough for today." Rudy cleaned and put away the clippers. Torrance opened the gate to let the sheep out.

"Let's go down to the house for some fresh rhubarb pie," Clara Belle said, dusting off her pant leg. As they walked down to the ranch house, Rudy's border collie ran up to greet Leah. As she did, the chickens in the yard scattered in all directions.

"Hi, Collie!" she said, stroking her black and white head. "Are you keeping watch over the ranch today?" Collie didn't much care for anyone visiting the ranch. She had bitten a couple of strangers, but Leah was the exception; she was always excited to see her.

The ranch was peaceful now; the animals were fed and content. The chickens clucked and ate corn in the yard while the rabbits lay in the sun, burrowing nests to relax in. The ewes and lambs grazed in the pasture. The faint ringing of bells could be heard as they moved from one patch of grass to another. The goats momentarily looked up from their grazing, and then Leah saw them: what she loved the most… the horses in the pasture. Her heart leaped with anticipation. The horses were out in the open meadow, away from the trees and creek, so that would make for a short hike. She decided to eat her rhubarb pie in the ranch house, and then head out before the afternoon storms rolled in. Her ride would have to wait a little longer.

Mom's Oatmeal Muffins

Ingredients:

1 cup quick-cooking rolled oats
1 cup buttermilk or substitute 1 cup nondairy milk with 1 T. lemon juice
1 egg or egg substitute
1/2 cup packed brown sugar
1/2 cup vegetable oil
1 cup flour
1 teaspoon baking powder
1/2 teaspoon salt
1/2 teaspoon baking soda

Directions:

Combine all ingredients. Grease muffin pan or use paper cups. Bake at 400 degrees for 15 to 20 minutes.
Makes 12 muffins.
Optional: Add dates or walnuts. Eat with cranberry sauce.

CHAPTER 2

PEGAS AND THE BEAR

The Justs' ranch house sat on the edge of the hill and was built into it on one side, creating a cellar. Summer produce from Rudy's garden was stored there. Buried deep in a sand-filled barrel, carrots stayed fresh all winter long. The house had two stories and a big picture window that framed the ranch, the valley, and the mountains perfectly. Under the picture window was the kitchen table where Rudy and Clara Belle sat and told their stories, making history come alive.

The screen door squeaked and the door handle moaned as Leah turned it. The warmth of the kitchen hit Leah's face like laundry from the dryer.

"Hi, honey," said Clara Belle, as she reached her arms out to surround Leah with a loving hug. Leah smiled, greeted Clara Belle, and moved over to warm herself by the wood-cooking stove, which heated the entire house. The cream-colored stove had a flat area on top for soups, stews, and coffee, and an oven below for Clara Belle's breads and pies. The fire could be made on either side of the oven. A warming shelf hung above the cook top to keep the meal ready for the cowboys coming in off the range.

"How's the fire doing, Clara Belle?" Rudy took a special fork and lifted the circles on the cook top to add the log.

"Oh, it looks good," she said as he carefully placed the log into the raging fire below. The fire crackled as the flames hit the bark of the log.

"How would you like some fresh bread while you warm up?" Clara Belle handed Leah a slice of freshly baked bread dripping with butter. "I made it from whole grains and this grinder." Clara Belle pointed to a silver grinder that was attached to the wood-chopping block. Flecks of grain lined the floor surrounding the grinder.

"But that looks like horse feed!" Leah said, peering into the ten-pound bag of wheat berries. Rudy chuckled and poured his coffee. He set the pot back on the cookstove and grabbed a knife to spread rhubarb jam over his bread. Clara Belle always had something ready to eat: bread, potatoes, turnips, rhubarb pie, goat cheese, all freshly made and waiting to be devoured.

As Clara Belle sat down at the kitchen table, she paused for a minute and looked out at the valley below.

"Do you see what is different, honey?" Clara Belle asked, leading into a story. Leah looked around the room. The woodstove had hot coffee brewing on it, and the cuckoo clock was ticking. The table where they were seated had the same red-checked tablecloth. Colorful, cheerful Fiesta dishes lined the open shelves in the kitchen, reminding Leah of all the scrumptious things Clara Belle served on them. The living room opened up into the sunroom where Rudy and Clara Belle's beautiful plants were in full bloom. Fuchsias were her pride and joy, although she could grow anything. The entire house contained treasures of yesteryear and profound symbols of who these people were. Leah was stumped, though. She couldn't see anything out of place and couldn't figure out what was different.

"My mama used to tell us kids to pay attention to what the land is trying to reveal," Clara Belle began. "You can learn a lot about what is going on by the small signs that most folks miss. My mama was a Cherokee Indian. Her mama taught her this prayer which has been passed down through many generations and was written by Lakota Chief Yellow Lark in 1887." Clara Belle looked at Leah with a smile as if she remembered her own mother whispering the prayer to her. She threaded her fingers together and began in a slow voice that was almost like singing...

> *O Great Spirit,*
> *Whose voice I hear in the winds*
> *And whose breath gives life*
> *To all in this world:*
> *Hear me.*
> *I come before you, one of your many children.*
> *I am small and weak.*
> *I need your strength and wisdom.*

Let me walk in beauty.
And may my eye ever behold the red and purple sunset.
Make my hands respect the things you have made;
My ears sharp to hear your voice.
Make me wise so that I may know the things
You have taught my people.
The lesson you have hidden under every leaf and rock.
I seek strength, O Great Spirit,
Not to be superior to my brothers,
But to be able to fight my greatest enemy, myself.
Make me ever ready to come to you,
With clean hands and straight eyes,
So when life fades
As a fading sunset,
My spirit may come to you without shame.

Leah sat quietly, thinking of Indian life on the plains with their horses, teepees, and hunting parties. She imagined the smoke billowing out from the fire rings, the women busy doing their work, and the hunting parties parading around the camp with the day's kill: everyone searching for what they could do to bring honor to the tribe and to be the best they could be.

"So, do you see what is different?" Clara Belle asked with a huge smile, pulling her away from her thoughts. Leah's checks burned with embarrassment, and she shook her head.

"Well, honey, take a look at the small things in nature. Do you see life waking up after a long winter? New growth is starting on the plants. Animals are being born. Everything is becoming alive again." Clara Belle explained, "It was this time of year that my mama once had a visitor, an Indian from the North Country. He ate supper with her, and then, as a gift, he went down to the creek, cut several willow branches from the creek's bank, and sat right down and made a basket out of those branches. My mama said it was so beautiful to watch him work. The branches were soft, you see, as they are this time of the year. Early spring is a good time to weave willow branches into baskets before they dry out and get too hard." Clara Belle got up and picked up a basket that had been resting next to the pink blooming fuchsia. "This beautiful basket is over a hundred years old."

"Wow, that was made from the willow branches like ours?" Leah asked in disbelief. Off in the distance, she could scarcely see the tender new leaves coming out of the willow branches. Grass was starting to grow in the meadow with a few early wildflowers making their way up through it. Pole Creek raged dangerously high with the spring thaw of the winter's snow. Lambs ventured a little bit farther from their mothers as they grew more confident. The air felt crisp and cool, yet to be filled with pollen and mosquitoes.

"You're right, Clara Belle, the land does have plenty to say." Leah mopped up the remaining butter with the last of the bread and took the plate to the sink. "I'm going to go get my horse Pegas and head out," she said. "I'll see you all later."

Leah waved goodbye to Rudy and Clara Belle and walked, deep in thought. *Never again do I want to miss what the earth is telling me.* Leah paused to let a chicken go by. *I want to notice everything like the best Indian tracker. I want to bring honor to my family and be the best that I can be. I have to stop and listen to what nature is saying.*

All seven of the horses were now standing in the trees at the edge of the meadow, their favorite spot in the horse pasture. Leah slid the log latch and opened the gate. She walked down the hill to the valley floor and crossed Pole Creek on a single-board bridge. The water was running so fast and high that it almost covered the board. The rusty barbed wire fence was the last barrier into the horse pasture, and Leah took care to pass through it. Gently, so as not to prick her fingers on the barbs, she pushed the wire down just enough to fit through the fence.

All the horses raised their heads at once as Leah walked toward them, her feet squished in the wet grass. The two buckskin horses in the pasture were the Justs' horses. They were tan in color and had black legs, black manes, and black tails. Buck was Rudy's horse and he had a single white star on his forehead. He acted as if he was the boss of the herd. With his ears pinned back and his teeth showing, he charged anything, or anyone, that got too close to him. Horses ran to get out of his way. Leah steered clear of him too, so as not to agitate him.

Nubbins, Clara Belle's horse, was the other buckskin in the pasture. Nubbins was dappled tan and had a blaze with three white socks. She was much nicer than Buck. A small bay stood next to her.

"Would you like a cookie today, Spice?" Leah reached as far as she could to offer Spice a cookie. She put her ears back, flared her nostrils, and walked off. Spice was bay with a long star and two white socks on her back legs. She was Leah's first horse. Leah thought Spice looked like the horses in Western movies. She imagined herself riding to town to get supplies just like the cowboys did. Spice had had a baby named Sunshine in the early spring. The baby was frisky and mischievous at the same time. He had a sweet little muzzle with long whiskers growing out of it. He was named Sunshine because his mane was golden when the sun shone through it. Within the first few weeks of his life, Sunshine contracted Navel Disease and died.

"It's okay, girl. I know you are still sad. It will just take more time before you will accept a treat from me." She threw a couple of cookies next to Spice's front hoof. "I wanted to watch the baby grow up too," she said and turned to the rest of the horses.

Each horse asked for a "horse cookie" with their eyes and ears, but it was Pegas that Leah went up to.

"Hi, boy, how are you doing, today?" She threw the reins around his neck and took time to kiss his soft muzzle. He had a pink triangle under his chin and long whiskers that were yet to be trimmed. She bent down and put her cheek next to his.

"Awww, that wonderful, unique horse smell. You have perfume on today, Pegas!" She smelled his cheek. *Why do horses smell so good?* she wondered. *It must have been the sweat that accumulated under the cheek strap of the bridle.* She took a minute to savor the smell and hug his neck.

"You are my little Indian pony, eh, Pegas?" "Pegasus" was Leah's second horse and the son of Spice. He was a rare dun Appaloosa with a white blanket over his hindquarters and white spots that dotted his chest. He had a black-and-white mane that had so few hairs in it that it was roached short in the summer. His tail looked like a cartoon stick with a few hairs dangling off the end of it. The fly season was especially hard on Pegas. He whipped his tail around in disgust, but did not hit any of the horseflies that plagued him. Pegas was a uniquely colored Appaloosa, the chosen breed of the Nez Perce Indians.

Leah turned to Pegas, kissed the white spot at the base of his ear, and draped the bridle over his head. She put her thumb in his mouth so that he would take the bit, and then pulled it on over his ears.

"Come on, Pegas, let's go find a stump." Leah led him to the edge of the meadow where the tree line started. An old stump stood at the edge of the trees. "Without a mane, I can't swing up on you, now, can I?" She stroked his neck and stretched to get on. "Bareback with a bridle, and we are ready to go." She clucked to him and headed out across the pasture to the gate. She took a deep breath and sighed. "To be on the back of a horse, again." She trotted him up to the horse barn where her bareback pad was stored.

"Let's get you cleaned up." Leah bounced to the ground and quickly groomed him with a currycomb and a brush. With force, Leah flicked dirt out of the hairs on his back, careful to get the saddle area especially clean. Dust surrounded him, making it hard to breathe.

"Here you go," Leah said, putting the bareback pad on his back. She pulled the nylon cinch as tight as she could and took him to the side of the grain bin and hopped on the concrete foundation that was raised about two feet off the ground. She reached down to grab the willow branch Rudy left for her. Lightly, she tapped Pegas on the hindquarters to move him over.

"Come on over, boy." She encouraged him to take steps closer to her so she could get on. He moved a couple of steps closer to her. She hopped on and dropped the willow branch next to the grain bin.

"Hmm, where shall we go today, Pegas?" she asked as they walked away from the grain bin.

"Where are you two off to?" Rudy asked, carrying a feed sack out of the barn.

"I think we'll head up to Nine Mile Mountain and Sage Brush Point," Leah said, knowing it was important to let someone know where she was going. "That is one of my favorite rides."

"Well, be careful, now. It is a remote area and there are a couple of bears that live on the top of the mountain. It is springtime and they are looking for food," Rudy said as Leah's eyes widened in fear. "See you in a couple of hours," he assured her.

Leah headed out of the ranch, and up the draw to Nine Mile Mountain. Pegas softly walked along, knowing his job. The valley was spectacular with Pole Creek running through it.

"Easy, boy." Leah stopped Pegas to take in the sights. Green tree-lined meadows drew up to the magnificent mountains of the Continental Divide. The Divide looked like a big dam holding water from spilling over to the other side.

"Pegas, did you know that the Continental Divide is called that because rain or snow that falls on the eastern slope of the Continental Divide flows to the Atlantic Ocean, while rain or snow that falls on the western slope flows to the Pacific Ocean? It really does divide the water!" Pegas made no attempt to answer and was unimpressed with her knowledge. Leah twisted her body and, putting her hand on his rump, leaned back.

With a kissing sound and a soft leg, Leah turned Pegas around. "Let's go, boy." The narrow trail wound through pine trees and out into the meadow. Pegas hopped over small streams that crisscrossed the meadow, providing it with water. The trail widened on Nine Mile Mountain as she came into the aspen grove. It was a beautiful contrast of white aspen trunks with lush green grass and skunk cabbage below. Rocky Mountain Columbine popped their lavender and white heads up through the green grass floor. The tops of the green aspen trees were painted against the deep blue sky above.

"Whoa, Pegas, look at *this* view." Out in the distance, Leah could see the Continental Divide flanked by Snow Mountain and Byers Peak. "It feels like we are birds looking down on the mountains and valleys below." Leah leaned down and hugged Pegas around the neck. Pegas turned his head toward her to see if she had something to eat. "Okay, boy, here you go." She pulled a horse cookie out of her pocket and let him pluck it out of her hand. *Crunch, crunch, crunch.*

"Horses do love horse cookies!" she laughed.

Leah clucked to Pegas and turned him down the path across Nine Mile Mountain to Sage Brush Point. The hillside was covered with pine trees and the trail crisscrossed a couple of times up a steep hill to the top of the clearing.

As Leah neared the top, she stopped Pegas. "Hold on a minute, Pegas." She took in a deep breath. "Do you smell the cinnamon bush? It smells just like a candle." Leah sat sideways on Pegas and took another deep breath. "It sure smells good."

She continued to Sage Brush Point and looked out over the valley for a moment, then flipped her leg over Pegas's neck and continued down the trail. The trail off Sage Brush Point was down a steep ravine that had high banks on either side. It was so steep, that Pegas had a hard time keeping his balance as his back legs folded up behind him. One step at a time down the steep hill he went. His hips swung with each exaggerated step.

"I know it is hard going, Pegas, but the draw will open up into a sage brush clearing below in no time," Leah promised him.

Just as the trail flattened out, Leah heard a scratching sound ahead. Pegas heard it too. He stopped abruptly, raised his head, and pricked his ears forward.

"What is it, boy?" Leah whispered. All the focus was on the trees. Leah could hardly breathe because her heart was beating so fast. "*What is that noise? What's ahead?*"

At the same time, Pegas and Leah saw it. A black bear scampered up a pine tree right in front of them. For a moment, the bear's gaze met Leah's as he looked directly into her eyes. His long, sharp claws gripped the tree. Pine bark fell to the ground with each step up the tree he took. With barely any aids to encourage him, Pegas spun around and galloped up the same steep ravine he had just worked his way down, but he couldn't get his feet under himself in time, and went down to his knees while his head and neck went forward. Pegas groaned in pain and fear, his eyes wide open.

"Whoa, Pegas!" Leah screamed as she flew through the air, gone from the safety of his back and onto the bank. She slid on her side as pain shot through her shoulder. Within an instant, she sprang to her feet just as Pegas was getting back on his.

I have to get on before the bear comes after us, thought Leah in a terror. *The last place I want to be is on the ground or left behind with a bear nearby.*

"Easy, boy," she said as she ran up next to Pegas's neck. He was in a panic, walking fast with his head held high. She grabbed the reins, and in one move that took all of her energy, she grabbed the handle loop on the bareback pad and swung her legs up to his back. Pegas took off running, and with the forward motion, he propelled her in the air and she landed slightly behind the pad. Unable to grip his back, she bounced right and left with his strides. As the trail got steeper, his leaps got bigger, and with each leap she scooted herself in place and leaned forward. Lying on his neck, she wrapped her arms around him, hoping to not be dislodged again. He ran as fast as he could go. His breaths were deep and hard. His nostrils flared.

He ran up Sage Brush Point and down the other side before he felt comfortable enough to slow down. While still lying on him, Leah reached down Pegas's neck and stroked it. "Are you…okay, boy?" she asked. His head turned toward her slightly. His eyes were wide and his ears flicked back and forth frantically. His nostrils were big and red and had small streams of clear liquid coming out of them.

"You can relax, boy. We are safe now." For the first time since seeing the bear, Leah sat up. She turned to confirm the bear wasn't following them.

"That bear is probably still up in that old tree and just as scared."

Leah thought of nothing but the bear as she jogged Pegas the rest of the way home. She peered into every shadow and turned to look over her shoulder, just in case. Pegas did too. He looked extra hard at every tree trunk, stump, and twig that broke. Pegas had the smoothest jog of any horse she knew and when he was relaxed enough, he would grunt out a song to the steps of his silky smooth jog. Sometimes he actually fell asleep, stumbled, and caught himself before falling, but not today. That bear had scared him, and he was more alert.

The ride back seemed short. They were both exhausted. It felt good to be home in the safety of the ranch. Leah rode Pegas up to the horse barn and pulled the bareback pad off him. After a quick groom, she led him down to the horse pasture.

"Good boy," she said as she slipped off the bridle and gave him a horse cookie. He grabbed the cookie and trotted off, whinnying for the other horses.

Slowly, she turned and headed back up to the horse barn. Her legs were still weak. *Squish, squish, squish,* the water moved from under her feet. Carefully, she passed through the barbed wire fence, across the river on the board, and up the steep hill to the grain bin. Pushing the door in with her knee, she opened the door and put her bridle in.

"Well, did you two have an adventure today?" Rudy said, closing the door for her. Leah could only crack a smile and nod her head. She sat on the side of the grain bin and told him the whole story, hoping he wouldn't pass it on to her mom.

"Remember, we live in their home. That bear was in the tree because he was afraid of you." He put his arm around Leah. "Come on, I'll give you a ride home."

Leah was relieved as she climbed into Rudy's faded red 1965 Chevrolet pickup. She settled on the saddle blanket seat covers. Her legs welcomed the rest. They ached and throbbed more than usual. She didn't mind, though. Tomorrow would be another riding adventure at the Just Ranch.

WHOLE WHEAT BREAD

Ingredients:

2 cups whole wheat flour

2 cups all-purpose flour

1 packet instant yeast (~1 tablespoon)

1/2 teaspoon salt

2 teaspoon maple syrup

2 cups warm water

Directions:

1. Combine flour with the yeast and salt.
2. Dissolve the maple syrup in the warm water and then add to the dry ingredients.
3. Mix—don't knead—until dough is sticky and well combined.
4. Transfer to a greased 9" × 5" loaf pan.
5. Cover and leave to rise for 20 minutes.
6. While the dough is rising, preheat the oven to 390°Fahrenheit.
7. After rising 20 minutes, bake in the oven for 40 minutes.

CHAPTER 3

THE SPOTTED FAWN

The smell of the pine trees was invigorating as the last of the snow melted from around the house. Mud was everywhere. Snow covered the ground for almost eight months, but now it was springtime. Leah pulled her galoshes on over her cowboy boots and headed out the door.

After the long winter, the excitement to see the horses was almost too much for her to handle. It made it easier to walk in those heavy boots, though. The mud oozed from her footprints as she made her way down the dirt road to the Just Ranch.

Smoke from the old wood cookstove drifted out of the chimney as Leah stepped into the ranch house.

"Hi, honey." Clara Belle hugged her and pointed to a box on the floor. "Look what we have." The box was the size of a TV and had the words "Billy Cook Saddlery" printed on the side in red.

She walked over and peered in. There inside the box was a tiny, sweet lamb. He looked up at her with his brown eyes. He had a black face. His skin was wrinkled and gave little indication of the long wool that would grow later that summer. He was lying in the box, curled up on a blanket with a heat lamp shining on him for warmth. The lamb greeted her with a *"baaa."*

"Oh, how precious!" said Leah. "But what happened to him? Where is his mother?"

"I don't know, honey," said Clara Belle. "His mother gave birth to two lambs… twins…and for some reason she rejected one and claimed the other." Clara Belle turned and pulled a dishtowel off the hook. "But he is safe with us now. We will take care of him," she said, stroking his head. "Would you like to feed him?"

"Yes!" Leah jumped out of the seat. Clara Belle took a bottle of milk out of the water that was heating on the woodstove. She dried it off with a dishtowel and handed it to Leah.

"Be sure to tip it up," she warned.

Leah clutched the bottle and pointed it down toward the lamb's muzzle. "Here you go, little guy," she said. The lamb grabbed at it and pulled the nipple into his mouth. He lunged at the bottle a couple of times and almost knocked it out of Leah's hands.

"What is he doing?" She struggled to keep a hold of the bottle.

Clara Belle explained, "Why, when he is nursing his mama, he knows that he needs to punch her bag a couple of times to stimulate the flow of milk. He doesn't know the bottle is any different."

The lamb sucked the milk so fast that foam dripped from his little muzzle. His belly got bigger and bigger while his tail wagged back and forth.

Leah laughed. "I didn't know lambs wag their tails!" As the lamb finished, he licked his lips and wobbled back to his bed. He looked dizzy from the satisfaction of being fed. He lay down and went fast asleep.

Rudy sat at the table and stroked Tom. As his name implied, Tom was a tomcat. He was solid gray and had white under his chin and belly. He loved Rudy and would sit for hours on his chest, "hugging" him, with his paws stretched out on each of his shoulders. Every spring and fall, he would leave the ranch for a week's worth of hunting and exploring. Sometimes he would be spotted in Granby, which was seven miles away. When he finally came home, he was thin and was missing hair in a few places. He looked like he had been in a couple of fights. Every time, however, he would come back eager to be in Rudy's lap. Purring with delight as he was rubbed from head to toe, drool could be seen dripping from the corners of Tom's mouth.

"Leah, come look at this," Clara Belle whispered. This time she knew what she would see. Leah heard them before she saw them. *Cheep, cheep, cheep.* Baby chicks. They were little soft yellow fuzz balls running around. Leah gently picked one up and held it next to her cheek. The baby chick snuggled into her.

"These chicks were hatched in our incubator," said Clara Belle. "After the chickens laid the eggs, Rudy put them in the incubator, which kept them warm. Three times a day, we turned the eggs, and twenty-one days later, the chicks hatched." She picked one up and stroked it on the head. "When the chicks are old enough, they will get turned out with the older chickens, free to roam the ranch, feeding on the corn that Rudy spreads out for them."

Leah played with the chicks for a little while. The box contained water in a little dish and feed in an old ice cube tray. The heat lamp swung a few inches above them. Leah put her hand in and let them jump and peck on her. Gently, Leah picked up a chick that was standing in the corner and stroked the soft down on her belly. The chick stood up tall and flapped her wings.

"Does that feel good?" she asked the chick. She held it to her cheek one last time, gave it a kiss, and put it back down in the box, convinced that she had petted and played with every chick there. Leah hugged Clara Belle.

"We'll see you later," Clara Belle said as Leah and Rudy put their boots on and grabbed their jackets. They walked out of the ranch house and into the yard.

"What are you doing now, Rudy?" Leah said, wondering if he had a chore that she'd like to help with.

"Oh, I have to go irrigate the upper creek," Rudy said pulling his galoshes up higher. "At night the beavers dam the water up, and every morning I have to open the creek up again so that the water can flow into the pastures."

Leah followed him as he walked over to the machine shop and grabbed a hoe. "The pastures need a good drink of water to start off the summer growth of hay right." He put the hoe into the trailer of a small John Deere tractor. Two shovels were already hanging out the back. "The hay season is short at this altitude," he continued, "and I only get one cutting. But that hay is so nutritious that no additional feed is needed throughout the winter.

"Say, are you going to the horses right now?" Rudy asked with a slight grin, knowing the answer. Leah nodded. "Well, I think I'll join you today." Leah's heart leapt. She loved to watch Rudy with the horses.

"That's great!" she said. "And I don't have to worry about mean old Buck charging me today," Leah said under her breath.

Leah and Rudy turned and headed across the yard to the horse pasture. The horses were at the edge of the meadow under the trees, their favorite spot. Leah and Rudy made their way down the hill, across the bridge, and through the barbed wire fence. Water was everywhere in the pasture and splashed from the bottom of her boots. It came from both melting snow and from Rudy's irrigation.

Rudy was dressed in blue jeans, a red flannel checkered shirt, jean jacket, and a cowboy hat. The horses loved Rudy and knew that he always had treats for them. As he crossed the creek and headed over to them, the horses had their ears up and looked as though they were smiling. They seemed to talk to Rudy with their eyes.

"Hey, now, how are you doing?" he asked, as if he received an answer. The horses, one by one, nuzzled him and with their lips worked a horse cookie out of his jean jacket pocket. Rudy stroked their heads and necks as he talked quietly to them. Rudy was the original "horse whisperer." He always said that he'd never be lonely as long as horses were around. Leah watched him talk to the horses for a minute, then turned to catch her horse, Dandy.

Mud and manure were caked on Dandy's coat, but Leah ignored it as she slipped the bridle on and looked for a log. She found one next to the fence and took Dandy over to it. After she positioned him just right, she climbed on the log and jumped on. With her boots full of mud, it took all the strength she had to spring on his back and throw her leg over. At last, she was on. She rode across the pasture to the gate. Rudy had already opened it and was waiting for her.

"Thanks for opening the gate," Leah said. "I am so glad I don't have to get on again!" She smiled at Rudy. "Come on, Dandy." Leah encouraged him to walk through the narrow gate.

"All right." Rudy could see her relief. "I'll meet you up at the barn."

Dandy was part Arabian and part Quarter Horse. He was chestnut with a flaxen mane and tail. The orange color looked beautiful against his milk-chocolate coat. He had a white blaze that ran the length of his face down to his muzzle and two white socks on his back legs.

When Leah arrived at the horse barn, she put the halter on Dandy and tied him up so that she could groom him. With the currycomb, she brushed him gently, careful not to hit any bony areas. The hair, in three-inch lengths, came off in handfuls and soon covered the ground.

"Here you go, girls," Leah said as she pulled the excess hair out of the currycomb. She noticed that robins were staked out in the trees nearby and eager to get some soft horsehair for their nests.

"Ah, it feels good to get this hair off, eh, boy?" Leah stroked Dandy's neck. "It's time to get tacked up!" Leah grabbed the thick Navajo Western saddle pad, followed by her beautifully hand-tooled Western saddle. She tightened the cinch, then buckled the back cinch and the breast collar. Finally, Leah was ready to ride. She had been cooped up all winter long and wanted to get out into the wilderness.

"Are you two ready to go?" Rudy asked, handing her the reins.

"Yes, we are." Leah led Dandy over to the concrete foundation at the grain bin and hopped on. "I am heading up to the waterfall today," she told him. "I'll check on the rhubarb patch for you. It should be about ripe."

"You do that, and be careful," Rudy reminded Leah. "There is a lot of wildlife out right now."

"I will." Leah turned Dandy out of the Just Ranch and down the Pole Creek Valley. She rode by the old Rowley homestead. Karl Just and Fred Rowley became friends when he was given "squatter's rights" to the land in the late 1800s. The homestead had a great view of the valley that opened up to the mountains. Fred built a ranch house, horse barn, smokehouse, root cellar, logger's cabin, and a Mormon hay stacker. It had been many years since anyone lived there, but his spirit still remained.

Like clockwork every spring, the Rowleys' rhubarb came up across the meadow. It was not tended by anyone, yet there it was, year after year. Rhubarb was hearty to grow at that altitude, and the Rowleys' rhubarb patch must have been a hundred years old. Clara Belle came to the patch to get fresh rhubarb for her pies.

"The Rowleys planted the rhubarb and used to sell pies to passing tourists," Clara Belle once explained. "The patch is still there, producing fresh, sweet stalks every year." Clara Belle's fresh rhubarb pie was yummy. It was sweet and sour at the same time and very creamy. Leah always hoped Clara Belle had pie waiting for her in the ranch house, even when she knew rhubarb was not in season.

Leah headed up the draw where the green grass changed to pine trees. The cold air from the Gold Mine hit her from the dark shadow of the hole in the mountain. The air was stale and felt haunted with Greitzer himself. Grambril Greitzer was a gold miner who dreamed of striking it rich. Like most folks, he dug and dug but never found gold. Some say it made him crazy. He kept to himself and took company with his pet porcupine.

The dirt trail narrowed, and Leah stopped to let Dandy munch on the remaining grass. She swatted a fly off his neck.

"Is that good?" Dandy snorted and shook his head at the flies. "Okay, let's go, boy." Dandy reluctantly pulled his head up and started down the trail to the waterfall, grass hanging out of his mouth. Willow branches grew out of the banks of the creek. The trail followed the creek and crossed it in a couple of places.

"Let's jump the creek, Dandy." Leah goosed him a little with her legs, and Dandy hopped over the small ditch. It tickled her tummy. Dandy trotted a couple of steps more and jumped over the water in a wider spot.

"Whee!" Leah delighted in the thrill of jumping. The trail narrowed and winded in and out of trees alongside the creek to the base of the waterfall. The air was moist and chilly. Large trees crowded in around Leah. Dandy could hardly move. The noise from the water rushing over the falls was loud. Rocks were covered with moss. Leah could feel the mist on her face.

"Easy, boy," Leah assured Dandy to stand still and leaned forward to stroke him on the neck. "Let's rest here for a while." Leah stretched back on Dandy and listened to the water. It was like a secret world for her, a place all her own. Dandy also relaxed his hind leg and lowered his head. The roar of the water was all she heard. Clouds rolled by, building an afternoon thunderstorm. Birds flew between the trees above.

Slowly, Leah sat up and gathered Dandy's reins. "Ready to go, boy?" She turned him around and headed back to the ranch. She was so relaxed after spending time at the waterfall. Leah felt the gentle sway in Dandy's back and quietly listened to his hoof beats, her eyes half closed.

Suddenly, Leah saw something in the grass. Desperately, she grabbed at the reins, pulling mane, air, and leather, all at the same time. She drew them up just in time to stop Dandy. Beautifully nestled in the long, green grass, a fawn lay with his legs folded up and his nose tucked into his body. He looked like a little package. White spots dotted the brown fur on his back and big brown eyes peered unwavering from underneath long eyelashes.

"Dandy!" Leah gasped. "You almost stepped on a fawn!"

Leah swung her shaky leg over the saddle and got off Dandy. She took the reins off his neck and bent down to get a closer look. The brown hair had perfect white dots that splattered his back. Long ears were lined with dainty white hair. His nose was wet and black. Then she realized the baby wasn't moving. His eyes weren't blinking. He was lying perfectly still. She stroked him to see if he moved. He didn't. She scanned the land around her looking for his mother.

"Oh no, something is wrong! What should I do?" Leah asked Dandy, hoping for an answer. "If I leave him here, a coyote might eat him. I had better get this fawn back to Rudy. He'll know what to do!"

She stroked his back of beautiful brown hair. He was so small. Carefully, she put her arms around him and scooped him up and carefully draped him across her saddle. Dandy was nervous about having an animal on his back, but he stood still for Leah. She gently put her foot into the stirrup and got on. Leah held the fawn between her legs and the saddle horn with the fawn's legs hanging over each side of Dandy. In one hand she had the reins, the other was positioned on the back of the fawn, calming him and holding him in place. Slowly, she rotated Dandy back onto the trail.

"Rudy can help the fawn," Leah said. "I know it."

Dandy walked on toward the ranch. One step, two, then all of a sudden, the fawn woke up. His eyes were open wide and there was a look of panic was on his face. His legs started thrashing wildly as he worked to get away. He slipped through Leah's arms and jumped off Dandy's back. She watched as he bounded into the woods. Within an instant, the fawn was out of sight, hidden by tall grass and aspen trees.

"Oh no!" Leah looked around. "How could the fawn go from helplessness and calm, to sheer panic and terror?' She replayed what had happened in her mind, trying to understand what the fawn did. "I'd better get back and tell Rudy. Good boy, Dandy." She turned Dandy down the trail and patted him on the neck.

As she made her way onto the ranch, Leah could see the small tractor and knew that Rudy had finished irrigating and was working on the worm beds. Leah rode Dandy down to meet Rudy and jumped off to talk to him. She could barely get the words out quick enough.

"Oh, I see." Rudy looked sternly at Leah, explaining, "For the first three to four weeks of its life, the doe tells the fawn to stay in one place. It is odorless and will lie motionless when danger is present. The doe stays away from the fawn, only returning to feed him. Otherwise her odor will give away the fawn's location to predators. She wants that baby to stay in the place where she left it and not move until she gets back."

Leah looked up at him in amazement. "No wonder he was not moving and looked so wide-eyed."

"Now, by disturbing the fawn," Rudy continued, "you have moved him so that his mother may have trouble finding him. And the scent left on him from you and Dandy might make the mother reject him altogether."

Leah's heart sunk. Tears welled up in her eyes as she looked at Rudy, trying to not cry. Her stomach hurt and whole body burned with anger at herself. She felt embarrassed that she had done something so wrong.

How could my good deed turn into something so horrible? she thought to herself. She felt sick for the fawn and the mother and wished she had never seen it in the first place.

Rudy saw the look of disappointment on Leah's face and reassured her. "A mother's love is very strong. She will find him and love him just the same."

Leah struggled to smile. She pulled the tack off Dandy and led him down to the pasture.

The walk back up to the horse barn was slow because of the relentless mud and the broken heart.

"I should not have bothered the baby. I didn't respect nature the way Clara Belle taught me," Leah said to herself.

Leah reached the ranch house and saw Clara Belle lying on her side in the grass. In front of her were two little goslings. Clara Belle looked up with a grin. Leah took a seat on the grass near Clara Belle. She watched as the two baby geese waddled around. Yellow and gray down covered their bodies. Their beaks and feet were gray and they nibbled at the grass. Not far away were the gosling's parents, honking quietly, reminding them that they were close by. The sting of disappointment over the fawn eased a little from Leah's mind as she watched the baby geese.

A curious kid came over, followed by another. The baby goats were born a couple of weeks earlier and anything at their level was fair game. Both kids were all black with white- and black-speckled ears, and they wobbled on skinny legs. They nuzzled Leah and tried to eat her straight blonde hair. They smelled her ears, licked her face, and jumped and played right in front of her. They made her laugh. Leah gave Clara Belle a hug and turned for home.

The walk home through the mud was long and hard, but her thoughts drifted back to the fawn. She hoped he was back with his mother. The reassuring words of Rudy rang in her mind and she wanted to believe that everything would be okay.

CLARA BELLE'S RHUBARB PIE

Ingredients:

4 cups fresh chopped rhubarb
1 1/3 cups sugar
6 T flour
1 T butter
Double piecrust

Directions:

1. Prepare piecrust for bottom of the pie.
2. Combine sugar and flour together, then sprinkle 1/4 of the sugar mixture in the bottom of the pie shell.
3. Mix rhubarb with remaining sugar mixture, then add to pie.
4. Dot with butter.
5. Add top crust and trim the edges. Add slits to the top crust.
6. Place pie on the lowest rack. 450 degrees for 15 minutes, then 350 degrees for 40–45 minutes.

CHAPTER 4

PRANKS, DUDES, AND MARSHMALLOW-EATING DRAFT HORSES

The bedroom window was cracked just enough to let in the morning chill. The birds sang back and forth to each other. It was 5:30 in the morning. Time to get the horses.

"Why can't birds sing like that when folks are awake?" Leah wondered as she slipped on her jeans, snapped the pearl buttons on her Western shirt, and pulled on her boots. She brushed her long blonde hair and tied it back into a ponytail.

"Do you have a Breakfast Ride today?" Leah's mom whispered stepping into her room.

"Sure do, and a hayride tonight. I won't be home until late." Leah tucked her hands into her sweatshirt and headed down to the Just Ranch to get Dandy. Although it was summer, it was cold in the early morning.

At the horse barn, Leah quickly groomed and saddled Dandy. Rudy was already up and spreading corn for the chickens.

"Hi, Rudy," Leah said, as she tightened the cinch.

"Hey there," Rudy said. "Another busy day at the stable?"

"Yes. Dandy will be out all day. I'll get him back after dark."

Rudy waved and continued his chores. Leah turned Dandy and rode up the draw to the livery stable, where she worked in the summertime. Tourists, or "dudes," as they were called, loved riding horses in the wilderness. One by one, they called to make their reservation, not missing out on their chance.

Through the trees, the stable came into view. The barn was a long, wood building with windows on either side for thirty horses. Mangers were under the windows and held hay and grain for the horses. A tack room was at one end of the barn. Saddle racks dotted the walls, and a large rotating saddletree stood in the middle of the room. One wall held bridles lined up on nails that hung in two rows on the wall. The grain bin was catty-corner and held ten sacks of fifty-pound sweet feed.

"Mornin'," Hank called from the tack room as Leah led Dandy into the barn. Hank was the trail boss who looked like he'd had years of experience with horses. His legs bowed under his Levis, his boots were scuffed, and his face was leathered with years in the sun. His eyes twinkled, and his smile could erase any bad mood. He genuinely liked people, and people felt it. They were drawn to him, just the same.

"Howdy," she said, as she could barely move her frozen fingers. He winked at her and cracked a grin.

"Look at this." Leah quickly tied Dandy up at the first manger and walked into the tack room. Hank grabbed a coffee can out of the grain bin. The can was used to grain the horses. Hank tipped the can up slightly so Leah could see inside. She gasped silently. Inside was a dead mouse. Some poor soul would find it later. He chuckled and put it in the grain bin. She smiled and shook her head.

"I'm glad I'm not on the receiving end of that prank."

"Come on, boys," Hank yelled at the other cowboys. The five of them saddled up and rode out to get the horses. They rode one mile down a dirt road to the horse pasture. Hank got off Peppy and opened the barbed wire gate. The horses spent the night in a large pasture to graze. In the morning, they were scattered in all directions. Hank banged on a metal pan that had been placed next to the gate.

"Come, babes," he said so that all the horses, even the ones in the far corner of the pasture, could hear him. In an instant, the horses lifted their heads from grazing and galloped toward Leah and the other cowboys who were standing at the gate.

"Jim, you take the lead today," Hank called out. Jim nodded and turned his horse toward the stable and started trotting. He was the lead wrangler who galloped in front of the herd and led them the mile or so to the stable. When the front horses caught up to Jim, he urged his horse into a lope.

Leah stood next to the gate as all the horses thundered through. They ran wild and free. None of them had halters on and their long manes flowed in the wind. She saw all colors: bay, black, paint, palomino, grey, sorrel, white and chestnut.

"Jesse and Cade, run midherd." Hank waved them on as the horses rumbled through the gate. The two wranglers took either side of the herd and ran at the same pace as the others.

The last of the horses made it through the gate, and Hank and Leah spurred their horses into a gallop. The dust was thick and made it hard to breathe. But Leah loved being in back. She felt like she had control over the entire herd, making sure that all horses made it to the stable. Occasionally, there was a *whooooop!* sound from one of the cowboys trying to keep a horse up with the herd.

"Get up there," they'd yell with an impressive voice. The horses knew the routine. Back at the stable was a pile of molasses sweet feed for them to munch on.

The wranglers closed the gate as the remainder of the herd ran into the corral. Dust swirled to the sky. The horses breathed hard, snorted, and shook their heads. The wranglers got off their horses and tied them up at the back end of the barn.

"Okay, let's bring 'em in," said Hank. He stood at the gate and let only a few into the barn from the corral at a time. Some horses were lame or tired and could not be worked. Hank knew them all and kept them as healthy as he possibly could. Only the strong horses worked.

The wranglers filled large coffee cans with sweet feed and carried three at a time to the mangers.

"Yuk!" Jesse screamed and through the coffee can high in the air. *Bang*—it came down with a thud. Grain went everywhere on the tack room floor.

"Okay, who's the wise guy who put a dead mouse in the grain bin?" Jesse asked, waiting for someone to step up. Leah caught a glance of Hank over her horse's back. He chuckled to himself and just kept brushing.

As the horses came in, the wranglers put their halters on and clipped them to the lead ropes that were tied to the mangers. With brushes in hand, they worked down the line, grooming each horse.

"I'll grab blankets," Leah said. She was the smallest of the wranglers and could not easily carry the heavy saddles. She put the blankets on each horse's back, while the other wranglers saddled them up.

As the horses were groomed and tacked up, guests arrived for the breakfast ride. It was a long ride to the meadow below the Just Ranch, where an outdoor breakfast was served. Most of the dudes were city slickers who "had not been on a horse for ages."

Their inexperience showed in the outfits they wore and their mannerisms around the horses. Slowly, the guests were matched to the best-suited horses.

"This lucky man gets Bud," Hank called out, pointing to the man in the striped shirt. Bud was a tall, lean bay that had very long, loose lips. He slobbered when the bit was put in his mouth.

"Ma'am, I'll sell you Comanche," Hank joked with the man's wife. Comanche was a paint horse with white and gray patches all over his body. His mane, from his ears to midneck, was white, and from midneck to withers was gray.

"Leah, you grab Smokey for this little girl wearing the beautiful purple boots," Hank said as the group snickered. Leah unwrapped Smokey's reins from his neck. She tightened his cinch and led him over to the line.

"Are you ready?" Leah asked the girl, who was clutching her mom, nervous to get on.

"Go on, it's okay," her mom encouraged her.

"You have the best horse in the stable," Leah told her. "He is the smartest and the smoothest. You will love him." Leah continued, "Smokey is such a fine pony that he actually belongs in the Pony Club, riding English with perfectly proper attire and his white mane braided up against his shiny gray coat." Leah reached down lifted the girl up.

"He keeps up well and always takes care of the children who ride him," Leah said, holding her thigh. "His job is to stay behind the lead horse." Leah turned and led Smokey to the front of the dude string. The girl relaxed a little and pulled at Smokey's mane.

"You, sir, in the cowboy outfit," Hank said, pointing to a man with a "greenhorn" look to him. "You get to ride Widowmaker." The man's smile turned to a look of sheer terror. Hank smirked to himself. "What's the matter, you don't want old Widowmaker?" Hank helped him up on the horse. "Why, he's harmless as a puppy." That joke never got old for Hank.

The rest of the guests were matched up to their horses: Patches, Shadow, Cinnamon, Dolly, Apache, Midnight, King, Lightning, and Max.

"Okay, riders, listen up!" Hank commanded the group from horseback. "Pull back to stop your horse, move your arm across the neck to the right to turn right, and across the neck to turn left. Try not to let them eat, and no rodeo business out there today!"

The guests smiled as their riding adventure began. Jesse rode the lead in the front of the ride while Leah brought up the rear. She watched carefully to make sure no one got their foot stuck in the stirrup or tried to pass the other horses. The dude string took its time winding through the trees and hills. It looked like a train winding its way down the dirt trail. Nose to tail, the horses carefully chose their path over rocks, downed trees, and small creeks. For the most part, the trees were lodgepole pine, but at one point on the ride, the air got more humid as a nearby spring bubbled up, and the trees changed to water-loving aspen.

Here it comes, Leah thought. *The worst part of the ride.*

Jim turned around in the saddle and yelled so everyone could hear. "We have to go through a bog here. Just let the reins out and allow your horse to find its own way through it."

The mud was deep and never dried up. The horses struggled to get through it. Mud suctioned their feet, which came up with such force that drops of mud were catapulted onto the horse's hindquarters and the backs of unsuspecting tourists. Sometimes the mud would pull a horseshoe off. All the horses floundered through, except for Smokey. He crossed to the right just before the bog, climbing onto a trail on top of a steep bank. There was no mud there, just a small stream to step over. Smokey did not get muddy.

"I wonder if he does that to keep clean or protect the kid," Leah mumbled. "Either way, he is one smart horse!"

Finally, the trail opened up to the valley. The meadow sloped slightly down to Pole Creek. The mountains towered in the background. They seemed close and powerful. The warmth of the sun hit Leah's face and she knew the painful chill in her fingers was almost a distant memory.

The guests dismounted and headed over to the breakfast area. The wranglers tied each horse up to a long rope stretched between trees. Leah loved to see the different colored hindquarters lined up in a row. The horses enjoyed the rest and relaxed in the morning sun.

The camp was set up on a flat spot with a small creek bubbling nearby. The fire in the pit crackled and raged with an orange glow. Steam from the coffeepot wafted up from the old-fashioned kettle. The grate of the fire screeched as Hank turned the large pans with pliers hanging from his belt.

"It's breakfast time," Hank said as he poured the pancakes onto the griddle. "We make 'em big here, so you'd better get ready." He chuckled as the guest's eyes widened in amazement at the size of the pancakes. They were as big as a dinner plate.

"Leah, your job today is to fry the eggs." Hank grabbed a hunk of grease and flicked it into the large cast-iron skillet. "Remember," he said, "when you crack the eggs, dip your thumbs in the grease." Everyone laughed at his joke. Leah knew he was only kidding; he just didn't want her to break any yolks.

It was so hot standing next to the fire. The three fire rings were separated in the middle to make two half circles, then stacked on top of one another, making the firepit waist high. Leah's sister Kacy cooked the bacon. The coffee percolated next to the fire below the cooking area.

"You know how to make Cowboy Coffee, don't you?" Hank asked the guests. Everyone's head shook no. "You put eggshells inside the coffeepot to keep the grounds down. What? You don't believe me?" Hank cocked his head and reset his hat. "Sure enough, there are eggshells in that coffee. Cowboys have made it that way for years.

"Can I sell you another one?" he asked the guests, walking around with a pancake on his spatula. "How 'bout you, sir? You still look hungry." The man put up his hand and waved him by.

When all the guests were fed, it was the wranglers turn to eat. Never did a breakfast taste so good as the one that was eaten outside, in the brisk Colorado morning. The cowboys sat in silence as they ate, stopping only to get a glance of the mountains with the morning sun hitting them.

Back at the barn, Leah, Jesse, and Hank helped the dudes off their horses. It was painful for them because the ride was long and they weren't used to it. They moaned and groaned as got off and tried to walk again.

"See you next time!" Hank grinned and waved to the guests.

Leah led Dandy to the water trough for a drink. All the horses made their way over to it. It was big and round; many horses could drink at the same time. Dandy took long sips of water. Each time he swallowed, his ears flicked forward slightly. Then he stopped, lifted his head, and started chewing. Green water drained from his mouth as the last bits of grass and slobber dropped into the trough.

"Is that good, boy?" she asked. Water dripped onto Leah's pants and boots. "Oh, gross, Dandy. Thanks a lot!" she laughed and let him back to the barn.

With the horses fed and watered, Leah took a moment to rest on the rocking chair that sat perched on the wood porch of the office. The office was a small building in front of the barn that looked out over the corral. The alleyways were built next to the corrals and used to put the dude string together. Piles of horse poop dotted the line. Leah couldn't stand looking at it knowing there was a job to be done.

"Jesse, do you want to scoop poop with me?" Leah asked, hoping he would grab the wheelbarrow from the back of the barn. Jesse was sitting on the step and leaning back on a post. He rolled a toothpick in his mouth and took a moment to think about it. His hat was tipped forward so Leah could not see his eyes.

"Sure," he finally said; his spurs rattled when he got up. Leah spun around and ran to get the shovels.

Scoop, dump, *scoop*, dump, *scoop*, dump, the team worked together, moving their way down the alley. It was relaxing to scoop poop, Leah thought, oblivious to what was going on around her, and rewarding to clean the alley. *Scoop*, dump, *scoop*, dump, *scoop*, dump.

Suddenly, she heard a scream, then a yell that moved into frantic conversation. She looked up as the cowboys were wrestling Hank down. Two guys grabbed his legs while three guys were at his head and shoulders.

"What's happening?" she asked, frightened that something was seriously wrong.

Jesse winked and said, "Birthday dunk." He threw his shovel down and ran over to help.

The cowboys moved in unison out of the barn while Hank squiggled and squirmed like an inchworm.

"Grab the gate," one yelled as they moved to the corral. Leah giggled and waited for the fun. It was Hank's birthday, and the cowboy tradition called for a dunk in the water trough. This same water trough was filled with horse slobber, pieces of grass, and occasionally a "green submarine" of horse poop. The cowboys moved closer to the water.

"Boys, I'll string you up," Hank yelled, in disbelief that they would actually carry it through.

"Yeah, we know," Jesse yelled back. "You're a real tough guy."

"One, two, three!" The cowboys swung Hank and dropped him in the middle of the trough. The horses backed up, spooked at the commotion. The cowboys held their stomachs and laughed loudly. Hank stood up and "washed" his hair in the dirty water. He was soaked. He stepped out of the tank and walked over to the porch, squishing and dripping as he went. He sat down, took off his boot, and turned it upside down. Water poured out of it. He shook his head as he put it back on.

Several rides kept the wranglers busy during the day, but finally the long afternoon gave way to evening and hayride time. The riding horses were herded down the road to the pasture, while Duke and Andy were getting ready to start their day. This team of Belgian draft horses pulled the evening hayride. Their coats were golden, and their manes, tails, socks, and bellies were all cream colored. Duke and Andy were professional working horses who knew their jobs well.

"You're so tall I can't even see over you," Leah said as she brushed Andy and combed his mane to the sound of him chowing down on sweet feed.

"Jesse, are you up for a trick today?" Hank yelled, stroking Andy's hindquarters.

"Yeah, I'd like to see him do it." Cade smirked, unbelieving. Jesse heard the tone of sarcasm in his voice and took up the challenge.

"Sure, I can jump up on Andy's back." Jesse nodded and smiled, confident he could squash the doubt of any naysayer.

Leah moved away from Andy while Jesse walked to the opposite end of the barn. He turned around to face Andy with a determined look on his face. Then with all his power, he took off running straight for Andy's butt, something you *never* want to do. With gymnastic precision, he jumped up and practically did the splits midair over Andy's large frame. He landed just over the rump and scooted the rest of the way to the back of the draft horse.

"Amazing," Cade said. "That horse must be eighteen hands tall."

"Told you I could do it," Jesse said, crossing his arms and puffing his chest out. Hank shook his head in sheer admiration. Andy just kept eating.

Leah caught a glimpse of the girl with purple boots sneaking a peek in the manger window, staring in awe at the giant head before her.

"Hi there, would you like to help me harness old Andy here?" The girl nodded her head yes. "Well, come on!" Leah led her into the tack room.

"First, we have to put this heavy collar around Andy's neck, buckle it, and make sure it rests on his shoulders." Leah struggled to get the leather buckled, then positioned it in place. Next, she went into the tack room and pulled the harness off the wall hooks. Starting at the back of the harness, Leah grabbed the rump safe and draped it over her arm, then she put the saddle over her forearm, and with her two free hands, she grabbed the wooden hames.

"These hames rest on either side of the collar and are what pulls against the horse," Leah said. "Let's try to get this harness up."

Leah closed her eyes and, with all of her strength, *one, two, three*, she threw the harness as far up Andy's body as possible. It only made it halfway up his body. One by one, she put the harness parts in place, each piece put where it belonged and strapped in. The hames were laid on either side of the Andy's neck and rested in the grooves of the collar. The saddle was strapped in just behind the withers, and the rump safe rested on top of the hindquarters. After the big pieces were set into place, all the straps were buckled down tight: the hames, the saddle, the quarter strap, and the hip strap. After checking everything a second time, Leah put the bridle on.

"Would you like to thread the lines through the harness?" she asked the little girl. She nodded her head. Leah lifted her up, and she threaded the long line through the keep.

"Now it's Duke's turn!" Leah said with a sigh, putting the little girl in the manger to watch.

After Duke and Andy were ready, Leah led them to the wagon.

"Back, back," Leah said, clucking to them. "Come on now, back up." Duke and Andy backed up to the wagon with the tongue in between them. Leah attached the tugs to the wagon.

"Easy, boys," she said, not wanting them to move while she was in front of the wagon. Once the horses were put into place, she exchanged the inside lines with each horse and climbed into the driver's seat. The guests loaded up onto the wagon and sat on the fresh hay.

"Is everyone ready?" Leah turned to ask the guests and make sure everything was secure.

"Duke, Andy." The horses stiffened, awaiting their command. Their ears flicked back and forth. "Okay, boys, let's go," she said. Duke and Andy braced themselves against the weights of the wagon and pulled the wagon down the road to the Rowley Homestead. *Clip, clop, clip, clop.* The team's hooves made a powerful sound on the dirt road while the tugs sounded like bells ringing. Leah sat just behind the team and watched their strong muscles work as they pulled the load. She held the lines in each hand and draped the slack over her shoulder.

Hank pointed out a large rut coming up in the road.

"You'd better crank 'em around that one," he said, wanting her to move the team to the right to avoid it.

"Gee, boys!" Leah yelled out. The tongue strained under the weight of the wagon as the horses moved to the right. *Clip, clop, ding, dong, clank;* the horses and wagon made many sounds.

"Haw, boys!" Once past the rough road, Leah moved the team back to the center of the road. *Clip, clop, ding, dong,* they moved closer to the campfire.

Leah turned off the main road and maneuvered the wagon between two trees.

"Whoa, stand," she said. Duke and Andy stopped at the campfire. The guests jumped off the hay wagon and walked over to the fire.

"Move on," Leah turned the team around and away from the campfire, stopping them before a big tree. She got down and tied them up.

As with all horses, Duke and Andy loved treats. The wranglers on a hayride, however, don't have many horse treats like horse cookies, carrots, or apples on hand. No, they had *marshmallows*! Not exactly horse treats, but Andy especially loved them. As soon as he saw the fire ring, he started asking for marshmallows with his eyes and ears.

"Here you go, boy." Leah placed her hand under his muzzle. His large, floppy lips struggled to find the soft marshmallow. His bit rattled as he worked it around in his mouth. Foam from his lips formed a sweet-smelling slobber.

"Here you go, Duke." Leah fed one to Duke. She didn't want him to be jealous. Eventually, he learned to love marshmallows as much as Andy did.

The fire ring was located across from the Rowley ranch house and had a pit in the middle of it. Large logs circled the campfire for people to sit on. The orange fingers of the bonfire reached for the black sky. Stars faded in the glow. The wood fueling the fire was a teepee with glowing orange embers below. *Crack, pop, crackle,* the flames broke the silence. The guests grabbed sticks and stuck marshmallows on, two at a time. The creamy confections were browned to perfection and put between two graham cracker halves and a piece of chocolate.

"*Yum*, now that was the perfect s'more," Leah said out loud as she licked her sticky fingers. She quickly ate her s'more and stood up to talk to the guests.

Leah explained the history of the Rowley Homestead and invited them to sing campfire songs. Everyone loved to sing campfire songs! *I love the Mountains, Kum ba Yah, Clementine, Home on the Range, She'll Be Coming Round the Mountain, Edelweiss, This land is Your Land,* just to name a few. Hank grabbed his guitar and set a melody.

The evening turned cool as the fire went out. The stars seemed brighter than ever against the dark night sky. Leah walked over to untie the team.

"Duke, Andy," she said, careful not to spook them. They had bridles with blinders on and couldn't see her unless she was in front of them. The guests loaded onto the wagon, lying on the soft hay, while the team headed back for home. It was dark, but that didn't matter. Duke and Andy knew where they were going, happy to be home after a hard day's work.

When the team pulled into the stable, the guests were unloaded and headed to their cars to go home. Leah unhooked the tugs and walked Duke and Andy back to the stable and hooked them to the manger. She unhooked the pieces of the harness and pulled it off, stacking each piece onto her arm. Leah carried the harness to the tack room and put it up.

"You got pretty hot tonight, didn't you, boy?" Leah felt Andy's wet neck. "He's lathered up, I'd better walk him out," she said to Hank.

"Sure, I'll grab Duke." Hank backed Duke out of the manger, and they walked around the corrals. Gradually, the horses dried off and cooled down until their heart rate returned to normal and their nostrils stopped flaring.

"Here you go, boys." Leah dumped hay into their manger.

"Are you going to be okay taking Dandy back to the Just Ranch?" Hank asked, concerned for Leah riding by herself in the dark.

"I think I have just enough light," she said looking up at the moonlit sky.

"I'll put Duke and Andy up, why don't you get started?" Hank said, leaning against Andy's hindquarters.

"Okay, see you tomorrow." Leah turned and untied Dandy. She decided to leave her saddle at the stable and ride him bareback home. That way, she wouldn't have to take it off in the dark.

Just as Leah thought, there was enough light for her and Dandy to see. She rode him down the road to the Just Ranch. There was a faint whinny when Leah opened the gate to put Dandy up. Despite the darkness, he turned from her and ran across the pasture to the other horses.

She turned and commenced the walk home. In the darkness, the stars shone brightly. She felt very alone, as if she was the last person on earth. A light breeze taunted her. She heard nothing. Her steps were choppy, as she could not see the uneven ground. She felt the eyes of a black bear looking at her. Leah sped up her gait and imagined being in her warm bed.

CAMPFIRE S'MORES

Ingredients:

1 sheet of graham crackers
1–2 marshmallows
1/2 chocolate bar

Directions:

1. Toast the marshmallows over the fire to golden brown, or burnt if you like it.
2. Break the sheet of graham crackers in half.
3. Add half of the chocolate bar on one half of the graham cracker.
4. Place the toasted, warm marshmallow on top of the chocolate.
5. Top with second half of graham cracker.
6. Smash down.

Eat while warm and gooey.

CHAPTER 5

SWEET CHEROKEE

Clara Belle waved the girls into the ranch house. Rudy sat at the kitchen table sipping a cup of coffee in one hand, holding his binoculars in the other.

"Hi, honey," she said with a hug. "Come on in." Leah kicked her boots off and pulled out the ranch chair to sit down. Clara Belle took a rhubarb pie out of the oven, cut a small slice, and placed it in front of Leah. Leaning over the plate, she took a long, deep breath, relaxing in the smell of her favorite food. She smiled at Clara Belle and paused to feel the warmth of the oven hitting her. The oven door squeaked as Clara Belle closed it, hushing the fire within.

The red-and-white-checkered tablecloth held bird books and nature magazines. A pair of black chaps hung on the ladder-back of the chair. The chaps were made of leather with silver brads that lined the edges. The letters "REJ" followed the curved corners at the bottom. Clara Belle grabbed them off the chair and held them up to her waist.

Leah turned to Kacy. "I have never seen anything so beautiful!" Kacy nodded in agreement, between bites of creamy rhubarb.

"Yes," said Clara Belle. "These are Rudy's chaps."

"My mama gave those to me when I was sixteen years old," Rudy said, pushing his black square glasses up the bridge of his nose. "She had them made in Denver and sent up on the train." He ran his hand over his initials. "I worked hard to earn them and she had to save a year to buy them." He grinned, youthfully, as if he remembered the day he was given them.

"When I was younger," Clara Belle said as she pulled a chair up and sat at the end of the table, "we used to wear chaps like these while running cattle high in the mountains. The cattle grazed on the tall grass near the creeks and wound their way through the forests."

Tom jumped on Leah's lap, stretching his arms up to hug her, looking for a back rub. He purred in contentment and drool dripped through the missing tooth in his mouth.

"When trees were down or the forest too thick, we rode next to the cows to get them out," Clara Belle continued. "Tree branches whipped at our legs. The hills were windy and steep and the mountain sun was relentless. We'd stop briefly for some bread and jerky, then headed out again. There were creeks and rivers to cross. The paths to different pastures were sometimes narrow and rocky, and both horses and cattle had a hard time passing. It took a long time to get them through, and cowboys had to spend hours on the back of a horse. They needed chaps like this to protect their legs." Clara Belle paused for a moment, and then looked up at Leah. "Is that the kind of adventure you are looking for today?"

"It sounds like fun. Boy, I would love to ride like that," Leah said. "It must have been hard work."

"I suppose it was, but I can't remember when I wasn't on the back of a horse. When I was a girl at home," she continued, "Daddy would never let us ride a horse with a saddle. When I could ride, stand on, or do anything I wanted to on a horse, I was old enough to get a saddle. Every time the cowboys left the ranch, they would leave a saddle for me. I'd pull the stirrups as high as I could to fit my short legs, and the next day, someone would come and let them out again.

"One day, Daddy came home with a saddle just for me. It wasn't a new saddle, but it was new to me, and I loved that saddle. An old Cherokee Indian who was staying on the ranch went and cut off some rawhide off a deer hide. He brought it back to me and said, 'Now, you lace up your saddle stirrups and no one will take them out again.' So I did, and that saddle just fit me."

Clara Belle knew what it was like to be a real cowgirl. Leah picked up the wooden picture frame sitting next to the table. It displayed a tough cowgirl with smooth Cherokee skin, short hair, and small figure. Clara Belle wore an embroidered buckskin shirt, leather beaded gloves with rawhide fringes hanging from the cuff, and a pair of dark chaps that fell to her ankles with long fringes on them that looked more like a skirt. Her rope was coiled in her hand, and her foot rested on a saddle that was lying on the ground. She gazed onto the prairie, as if checking the cattle.

"I bet you rode circles around those ol' cowboys," Leah said, holding the picture in her hands. "I would have loved to have seen that!" she said.

"Yeah, Clara Belle could do things with a horse that no other cowhand could." Rudy laughed, looking off in the distance through his binoculars. "That's why I kept her on as a ranch hand." Rudy lowered the binoculars and smiled at Clara Belle. "She's my sweet Cherokee."

Clara Belle giggled, her eyes narrowed and her cheeks rounded.

"I bet they didn't like having a girl show them up," Leah chimed in as Rudy once again raised his binoculars. "Rudy, what *are* you looking at?" Leah noticed how intently he was watching something in the horse pasture.

"Oh, Penny is just not right today. I want to make sure she's okay," Rudy said, his voice concerned.

"Is something wrong with her or the baby?" Leah held her breath and waited for bad news.

"I don't know," Rudy said, glancing at Leah, not wanting to alarm her. "I'll keep an eye on her today."

Leah felt her face warm up and fingers of fear grip her around her ears. Spice had lost her foal earlier in the year, and she didn't want that to happen again. Tears welled up in her eyes and she concentrated on not letting them spill over. Rudy half smiled at her, knowing what she was thinking.

Leah jumped up from the table, hugged Clara Belle, and then turned to her sister. "Kacy, let's go ride."

Kacy put Tom on the floor and gave him one last scratch on his back. She grabbed Rudy's chaps and held them up.

"Hey, how do I look?"

"You look like a tough cowgirl," Clara Belle laughed. Rudy smiled. Kacy took them off and hung them on the horseshoe hook that hung behind the door.

"We'll see you later. We're goin' to work cattle today," Leah said, winking at Clara Belle. She wanted to check on Penny for herself, get the horses, and begin her own cowboy adventure.

"Rudy, we'll take a closer look at Penny while we're down there," Kacy said, following Leah out the screen door.

Leah's horse, Dandy, was in the far corner of the pasture. She approached him and quietly slipped his bridle on.

"Hey, boy, how are you today?" she said to him softly and held out a couple of horse cookies. His lips encircled the cookies and he munched contently. "Get off there, you pesky fly." Leah flicked a huge summer horsefly off his neck. She split her reins and threw them around his neck. She grabbed his orange mane and swung up on his back.

"Kacy, look at Penny," Leah said, pointing to her large belly. Penny was a black horse who shone like copper in certain light. Although she was an Appaloosa, she had no spots, just white hairs hidden in her black coat. She had a small white star on her forehead and a sock on her left hind leg. Leah remembered the first day that Penny arrived at the ranch; her mom put the girls on Penny's back along with two other friends. There were four girls riding Penny all at once! That was a few years ago, and now Penny was pregnant and going to have a foal. The father was a beautiful red sorrel Appaloosa stallion with a white spotted blanket over his hindquarters.

"Is she okay?" Leah asked Kacy. "Does she look like the two mares you helped deliver with Doc Peterson last summer?"

Kacy led Brandy over to Penny. She ran her hands over Penny's belly and bent down to check her milk bag. "Should we go get Rudy?" Leah asked, with half her breath, the fear of losing another foal returning.

"She's waxing, all right," Kacy said. "It won't be long now. It might even be today." Leah clenched her fists and took a deep breath. "She's all right for now, but we'll want to check her when we get done riding."

"You know, we have to give the foal an Indian name if it has spots, just like the Nez Perce Indians," Leah said, turning Dandy toward the gate. "I hope it has its father's markings."

Kacy turned to Brandy, jumped up to her withers, and kicked her legs to get on. Brandy was sorrel and had a blaze down her dainty face. A faint handprint of white hair was stamped on her left hip. She looked mystical, as if Indians had tamed her. The girls rode to the horse barn and saddled up the horses. Kacy tied the brown saddlebags onto her saddle and stuffed their lunches into each side.

"Kacy, look at these." Leah pointed at a pile of old feed sacks. "Let's make our own chaps."

"Great idea!" said Kacy. Leah pulled a sack up and ripped a hole in the bottom. She pulled it over her leg and looped it under her belt. "How do I look?"

"Like a real cowboy," Kacy said. "I want one too." She pulled her sacks on and fastened them to her belt.

Once saddled, the girls set out. The summer air was fresh and clean. Wildflowers dotted the side of the trail. The sky was dark blue and void of any miserable thunderstorms. First up the draw and then over to Nine Mile Mountain they rode, two by two, unless the trail became narrow. The hills went up and down and around each corner was a new scent and view.

"Yeehaw," they yelled, twirling their imaginary ropes in the sky. "Get going, you little doggies," Leah said, laughing at their pretend cattle drive. She slapped her "chaps" to move the herd along. The trail widened into the meadow below the Rowley's Place. Leah kicked Dandy into a lope and headed off to the right to pick up some strays. Brandy did a pivot and raced back to push the herd forward. Leah stopped Dandy and stretched as far down as she could. A sunflower stood tall on the edge of the meadow. She examined it for clues and noticed footprints next to it.

"I think outlaws have been here," she said. "Let's be on the lookout for them."

Kacy gave the secret signal by pointing to Brandy's left ear and touching her left shoulder. Leah smiled and moved a handful of Dandy's mane to the other side of his neck. Quickly, Kacy reined Brandy down a bank and into thick brush. Dandy followed, careful not to be seen. A small opening in the brush led them through the aspen trees to the side of the creek. On the bank, trees created a perfect canopy from which they were hidden from outlaws and the afternoon heat.

"Do you think anyone saw us?" Leah asked, jumping off Dandy and tying him up.

"Nah, I think we're safe for now," Kacy said, pulling food out of her saddlebag.

"You can rest here for a while, Dandy." Leah picked a handful of grass and fed it to him before tying him up with a slipknot. She walked down to the creek and balanced on a log stretched across the stream. A couple of big gray jays rested on the branches of a tree. The "camp robbers" waited for any crumbs to fall.

"Let's eat on this log," Leah said, kneeling. "It's perfect, and we can put our feet in the water." Kacy followed her over and sat down. She took the food out of her sack and handed Leah a sandwich. Leah pulled her burlap chaps and boots off. She threw her socks in her boots.

"Thanks," she said, relaxing in the warmth of the day. "This is one of my favorite hideouts, so close to the Rowley homestead."

They lay on the log for a few minutes and snoozed. The creek babbled over the rocks and small flies buzzed above the water. A gentle breeze waved the leaves of the Quakies. The sun warmed them through the tops of the branches. Dandy and Brandy stood with their eyes half closed and their hind legs cocked, enjoying the rest.

Kacy pierced the silence with her voice. "We'd better get going if we want to beat the afternoon thunderstorms." Leah jumped up and looked at the sky. The clouds appeared without any connection or purpose, but sure to form a thunderstorm later.

"Yes, we probably should."

The girls loaded up the saddlebag that Kacy had on her saddle. "Let's head up to Blue Ridge Mountain," Kacy said.

"Will we have time before the storms arrive?" Leah asked, pulling her burlap chaps back on.

"I think so," Kacy said as she tightened the cinch, "but we'll need to hit the trail now."

"Hey, Dandy, it's time to go," Leah said and unclipped the lead rope tied to the tree.

"Come on, Brandy." Kacy led Brandy over to a large tree stump and hopped on. The horses were refreshed and popped out of the hidden entrance to the hideout.

"Did anyone see us?" Leah whispered, not wanting to share their favorite place.

"No, I don't think so," said Kacy, scanning the area. The two girls turned the horses up the old, dirt-logging road that led to Blue Ridge Mountain. Up ahead the dirt road turned to the right, while the horse trail cut to the left.

"Here's our turnoff," Kacy said, maneuvering Brandy to the trail that was overgrown with brush and barely wide enough for a horse.

"Glad we have our chaps on," Leah said as the brush ripped at the burlap covering their legs. In places, the trail was very steep and rocky. Slowly, the horses made their way up the mountain, heading in one direction, then the other, joined by steep switchbacks. The horses' sides heaved with each breath and their necks were wet with sweat. Finally, blue sky could be seen through the trees as they reached the summit.

"It has a lot of turns, but once on top, the view is worth it," Leah said, pulling Dandy up to look at the vista. The thick pine trees covering the hills opened up to the meadows in the valley below. Snow Mountain was on the right-hand side, the Just Ranch in the middle, and Nine Mile Mountain on the left. The Continental Divide rose out of the meadow's end. The patchwork of sun made its way through puffy clouds that accented each beautiful detail of the valley.

"Hey, you can see the Just Ranch from here." Kacy scanned out over the valley. "You can even make out the horses in the horse pasture."

Leah gasped, "Look, Penny is standing all alone." She knew what that meant. Penny was in trouble. Suddenly, a low rumble could be heard in the distance. The clouds were forming a storm at the end of the valley and moving right toward them.

"Let's go," Kacy said sternly and whirled Brandy around. Leah scrambled to sit square in the saddle again as Dandy followed Brandy without her. Within a couple of steps, Kacy disappeared off the ridge and back down the series of switchbacks. She knew the danger of being on a horse in a mountain thunderstorm.

"Going down is not much faster," said Leah, "and these storms are quickly forming." Kacy looked up in time to feel the first raindrop hit her head.

"Oh no, we need to get off this mountain and under cover right away!" Kacy yelled, knowing the lightning was coming soon. The huge thunderhead was building like Lego blocks in the sky; the gray underbelly getting darker and darker.

The girls urged the horses to speed up their steps as much as they could, going down the steep hill. They sensed the urgency. Finally the trail flattened out, and once on the dirt road, they loped the horses.

"We'll never make it back in time!" Leah was panicked. "The ranch is just too far away."

"We need to get to the Rowley Homestead before the lightning hits." Kacy pointed across the meadow. "We can take cover there." Leah pushed Dandy ahead. The sprinkling came steadier. Leah struggled to keep Dandy on the edge of the road in the soft dirt. Finally, the meadow came into view with the Rowley Homestead on the hill above it. Leah turned Dandy off the road onto the dirt path across the meadow.

Crack! Pop! Boom! The first lightning strike flashed around them, and thunder rolled down the valley.

Kacy screamed, and Leah crouched down low on her horse. She was riding low over her horse like a jockey, urging him to run faster. Running that fast, Dandy could easily step into a hole and break his leg or catapult over, but she couldn't think about that right now and had to keep pushing him.

"Mom will kill us if she finds out we are riding in lightning," Leah said under her breath. "We're the highest thing in this field, and with the metal horse shoes, we're a sure target for a strike."

Pop, crack, ka-BOOM! A swift lightning flash popped to the left of Leah and hit a tall pine tree on the edge of the meadow. In a full run, Dandy jumped at the noise and took a huge leap, as if he was jumping a wide stream. Leah screamed and grabbed his mane. Just as she did, Dandy slipped in the mud and went off-balance.

"Stay on," screamed Kacy. "If you fall off, we'll have to stop." With all her strength, Leah worked at pulling herself up. The bounce of the lope caused her leg to lose its grip. She felt herself sliding off, when the bounce of another stride put her upright and gave her a firm hold. She kicked her hanging leg, and got up in the saddle.

"Dandy, be careful!" Leah screamed and buried her hands in his orange mane.

The meadow flew by under the hooves of the horses, and in less than two minutes, they were at the Rowley's place.

"Follow me," Kacy said, running Brandy up to the horse barn and jumping off. She led her into the open doorway of the barn. "Whew, that was close," Kacy said. She slowly unclenched her fists, her hands red from holding to the mane so tightly.

"I can't believe how quickly that storm came up," Leah said, looking out the doorway. "We'll have to wait here a long time until it passes." The cloud burst and rain poured across the meadow. Swift flashes of light followed by unnerving thunder rolled down the valley.

"Oh, you know storms in the mountains of Colorado move through quickly. In no time the sun will be peeking through the massive thunderheads," Kacy said. "By the time the horses cool out, the storm will pass."

In a few minutes, she was right, and Kacy led Brandy out of the barn.

"Let's go check on Penny," Leah said, leading Dandy to the old tractor nearby. She climbed on the old fender and jumped on his back. The girls moved quickly down the valley to the Just Ranch, trotting the whole way. A beautiful rainbow appeared across the pastures as the sun broke out over the mountains. The air smelled fresh, and all of the pollen was washed from the sky, outlining leftover puddles in yellow.

Penny was now standing by the creek. Leah could see Rudy walking down to the horse pasture. He waited for the girls at the gate.

"Something happened!" Leah screamed to Kacy and galloped Dandy down the slope to the horse pasture. "What's wrong?" Leah asked Rudy, stopping Dandy right at the fence.

"Well, she just had the foal," Rudy said cautiously. "Let's go see."

As quickly as they could, the girls pulled off their saddles and laid them next to the gate. Rudy held the gate open as they led their horses through it, pulled the bridles off and hung them on the fence. They waded through the creek, balancing on any rock they could find, not caring if they got wet in the process. Penny was getting a drink on the other side.

"Hi, girl, did you have your baby?" Leah asked, running her hand down her shoulder.

"Over here!" Rudy called the girls over. The foal was nestled in the grass. She was alert and curious about her new visitors. Her ears flicked back and forth, and she couldn't decide if she should get up or not.

"Well, now, hello there," Rudy said kneeling next to the foal. Leah slowly knelt down on the other side of her, the grass still wet from the passing thunderstorm.

"Oh, you're magnificent," Leah whispered in her ear. She pulled her burlap chaps off and slowly stroked the foal's wet neck.

"She looks just like her dad," Kacy said, "a perfect marking for an Appaloosa."

The foal was solid black except for the white-spotted "blanket" over her hindquarters. Long whiskers came out of her muzzle and eyes. She had black eyelashes and fuzz coming out of her ears. A star took up most of the room on her forehead, and fluff from her mane was perched between her ears. She had long, spindly legs that were folded up underneath her. *Neigh*. Her delicate, newborn voice was adorable.

Leah saw Clara Belle walk up with clean towels and an apple for Penny. Rudy smiled at her as if the foal was his prized possession. He hugged her and took a towel from her.

Leah ran her hand down the foal's face and soft muzzle. She cupped her hand and the foal rested her muzzle in it.

"How sweet," Leah said. "You're *our* Sweet Cherokee."

Pinecone Craft Ideas

The woods are full of pinecones, so why not have some fun with them? Be sure to pick up ones that have fallen. Look for mature ones with their scales separated. Here are a few craft ideas.

Pet Pinecone – Glue googly eyes, stick tails, felt ears, paws and manes

Snowy Owl – Stuff cotton in between the scales, add googly eyes onto a felt face, add felt wings

Colored Yarn Ornament – wind colored yarn between scales, add a loop of yarn to hang

Pinecone Reindeer – On one end of the pinecone, glue googly eyes, a red felt ball for the nose and fabric ears

Pinecone Roses – Paint pinecones in bright colors, mount on top of green painted sticks, paint green leaves made out of scrap paper and attach to sticks, put into a clear vase.

CHAPTER 6

RIDE 'EM, SQUIRREL!

Nicki's ears flopped forward and her white tail curled up behind her as she put her head through the porch railings. Leah loved taking Nicki with her riding, but she always took a side trip to the dump where she dined on trash and got sick afterward.

"You have to stay here, girl," Leah said, giving her medium-sized mutt one last pat. Nicki was part spitz and basset hound who was plucked out of a laundry basket on the garage floor of an Oklahoma City suburb.

"We're going to the Just Ranch," Leah yelled to her mom, slamming the screen door behind her and Kacy. As the girls turned from the house, a bushy-tailed squirrel in a nearby tree sounded the alarm with loud, harsh chirps repeated rapidly, flicking its tail with every note.

"It's okay, little guy, we're leaving." Leah looked up at the squirrel, wondering why he was unusually agitated. Nicki gave a stern warning bark in the backyard that stopped Leah in her tracks. *Oh, that's why*, she thought and turned to investigate. Nicki was barking at the neighbor's cat. It was standing in the grass and would not move.

"How strange for the neighbor's cat to be in *our* yard," Leah said to Kacy. She yelled at Nicki to stop barking, and moved closer to the cat. A small squirrel was making a "swimming" motion in the grass. He was wet from being in the cat's mouth and was clearly injured.

"Get outta here!" Leah sprang forward and chased the cat out of the yard. She turned back in time to see Nicki open her mouth, about to enjoy a squirrel snack.

"Nickiiii!" Leah yelled and lunged to keep her from devouring the squirrel. Nicki took one last lick, and moved back. Leah was sure it was dead. Her stomach turned as she walked over to it.

"Hey, little guy, are you okay?" she asked, bending over to examine it. Her heart jumped when she saw that it was a young squirrel, and still alive. How badly was it hurt? she wondered. Was it suffering? Will it die?

"You're okay now," she said and picked it up. It was so small that it fit into her hand. The fur was wet from both the cat and Nicki, and it smelled like their slobber.

"Come on, let's go ride," Kacy said, standing impatiently with her arms crossed.

"Go ahead without me," Leah responded. "I'm not riding today, so I can take care of this injured squirrel."

"Fine." Kacy whipped around and walked away. Leah watched her go. For a split second she felt a longing to see her horse and hoped she hadn't made a mistake, then her attention turned back to the squirrel. "Phew. You need a bath." Leah went into the house and gently dried it off with a towel. It was whimpering and curled up in her hand. His coat was mostly gray except for the white outline around his black eyes. Its belly was white and its tail had long tan hairs in it. His soft teddy bear ears poked out of either side of his head.

"I know you're scared and don't want to be hurt anymore." Leah stroked its back. "I'll take care of you." Leah got him cleaned up and found a box to put him in so that he felt safe. She went to the horse trailer parked in the driveway and scooped up clean shavings for his bed.

"You look like a 'Hermie' to me," she said, and gently kissed him before lowering him into the box. A small container of water stood in the corner, but she didn't know what to feed him.

Leah jumped on her bike and raced down to the Just Ranch. Kacy was already in the horse pasture getting Brandy. Leah's longing to ride was gone, as she frantically worked to save the squirrel.

"Rudy!" Leah said with alarm as she walked into the farmhouse.

"What is it?" he said, sensing her urgency. He stopped slicing turnips and sat down at the kitchen table. She told him about Hermie, while Tom wrapped his arms around her and purred cheek to cheek.

"I see," said Rudy. "You should feed him a diet similar to what he eats in the woods. Squirrels eat fruit, grains, seeds, and nuts." He thought for a minute, and then went through the door to the storeroom. He immerged with a box of dry oatmeal baby food.

"Try this," Rudy said, handing the box to Leah. "We fed this to the injured ferret we had last month. Don't add water, just let him eat it dry."

"Great. Thanks, Rudy." Leah turned to head out the door.

"Keep an eye on him, and let me know how he does," Rudy instructed her.

"I will," Leah yelled as she ran to her bike. She pedaled as fast as she could to get home and check on Hermie. The squirrel was still asleep in her room.

"Here you go, little fellow," Leah said as she poured some dry oatmeal into a little bowl. Hermie smelled the food and seemed interested in it. He slowly sat up, took a flake of oat in his paws, and started eating it. He carefully ate the flake from all sides, spinning the flake in a circle. With each bite, his cheeks got bigger and bigger. When he finished with the first flake, he grabbed another and continued until he got his fill.

That night, she moved Hermie's box next to her bed. "Please, Hermie, please don't die on me tonight," Leah whispered to him. A tear splashed down on his box. "You are so weak." Her face heated up with the sadness she felt for this little creature. He moved in a circle trying to get more comfortable, and whimpered in pain. "I'm sure you have a family that misses you." She smoothed his tail. "I'll be your family for now." She drifted off to sleep, full of sorrow. A couple of times she was aroused by him wrestling in his nest, but otherwise, he was quiet all night.

The next morning, Leah nervously leaned over her bed to check on Hermie. He looked up at her as she looked down on him. "Oh, well, good morning!" Gently, she picked him up and held him next to her check. He seemed to submit to her and accept the fact that she wasn't going to hurt him. She laid him on her stomach and stroked him with her fingers. He watched her but didn't move a muscle. Her stomach growled, so she nestled him in the soft covers and went to the kitchen for breakfast.

"How's Hermie?" her mom asked.

"I think he'll be okay," Leah said, pouring a bowl of cereal. "I let him out. He's on my bed now."

"Oh no," her mom gasped. "You shouldn't let him out. He might get hurt or eat something he is not supposed to." With that, Leah threw down her spoon. She and her mom ran to her room. Slowly, they opened the door and saw him at the same time. Hermie was curled up next to her pillow sham, sound asleep. His eyes were black slits against the white hair that surrounded them. He held his tail with his paws, much like a baby blanket. They tiptoed back out of the room so as not to disturb him.

Leah went back to the kitchen to finish her breakfast, but angry humming sounds interrupted her. The hummingbirds were swarming and fighting around the feeder. Different tones from their beating wings made a language all their own. The feeder was empty, and the dominant, rust-colored rufous hummingbird was enraged. He fought the other birds off the feeder and tried to take the last of the sugar water for himself.

Leah held her breath and pushed her way through the birds, hoping not to get stabbed by their long beaks. She lifted the feeder off the nail and went to fill it in the kitchen. Leah's mom was ready with the feed. "One part sugar to four parts water." When she returned with the feeder, order had been restored. Beautifully colored hummingbirds sat on the red feeder flowers and enjoyed their meal. Even the rufous was more content and let the others drink.

She cleaned up after breakfast and went to check on Hermie. This time when she opened her door, Hermie was awake. He swiftly jumped off the bed and ran to her feet.

"Hello, Hermie, did you have a good nap?" Before she could pick him up, Hermie scrambled up her leg and sat on her shoulder.

"Mom!" Leah tried to yell softly so she wouldn't startle Hermie. "He thinks I'm a tree."

"*Amazing*. He has really taken to you." Hermie ran into her hair, barely visible to her mom. "I think you have a pet squirrel."

After a few days, Hermie seemed to be feeling better. Leah took him out of the box for lazy naps in the afternoon. He curled up on her bed. She read books to him. She showed him her Breyer horses and played with them on the floor. Day after day, Hermie stayed close to Leah, not wanting to be alone. With any loud noise or strange animal, he buried himself in her long, blonde hair and snuggled next to her neck. They became inseparable.

"Come on, Hermie." Hermie turned and ran up Leah's leg and sat on her shoulder. She went out to the kitchen.

"Mom, do you think I could ride with Hermie?"

"Sure, I think you could try," her mom said, mixing the batter of chocolate chip cookies. "If he runs off, then that is fine. He is strong enough now and can survive on his own."

"Are you feeling better, Hermie?" Leah asked as she stroked his back. "How about a ride?" Hermie turned to look at her.

"Mom, I'll see you later. Save me a cookie," Leah said, and headed out the door to get Pegas, with Hermie perched on her shoulder. Slowly, she walked down to the Just Ranch and into the horse pasture. The horses were just at the tree line.

"Hi, Pegas, we have an extra rider today. Meet Hermie," Leah said, walking up to Pegas, but he was more interested in the horse cookie that she was feeding him. Hermie stayed hidden in her hair. Leah slipped the bridle and bareback pad on and led Pegas up to the grain bin to get on.

"With the high concrete foundation, I can just step on," Leah said. "I don't want you to fall or get scared when I get on." She stepped up onto the concrete foundation. "Don't worry, we won't be galloping today!

"Come on over, Pegas." Leah grabbed the willow branch and tapped Pegas on the outside hip, asking him to move closer to her. She lifted her leg over his back and scooted on. Hermie was secure on her shoulder.

"Well, now, I see you have an extra passenger today," Rudy said, walking by with his hoe. "He is a very lucky squirrel." Leah smiled and headed down the road, out of the ranch. Hermie didn't move.

"Pegas is the smoothest horse, Hermie, so you'll be fine." Leah turned Pegas to the open valley near the Rowley Homestead. "We don't want to take go too far away, in case we have a problem."

The valley view was especially beautiful as it had been a few days since she'd ridden. Leah smiled at her mountain friends, mesmerized by their beauty. A movement ahead caught her attention, and she noticed hikers coming up the trail toward her.

"Is that...? No... Is that?" The voice of a man snapped Leah into reality.

"Is that a...a squirrel?" said the women. The hikers had spied Hermie and were in disbelief as to what he was.

"That can't be a squirrel," the man said.

"But it *is*!" said Leah, ending the debate. "This is Hermie. He was injured and I nursed him back to health. Now, he is my riding partner."

"Wow, that's incredible!" the woman said.

"That's somethin' ya don't see every day!" the man chuckled. "Ride 'em, squirrel!"

Later that afternoon, when Leah and Hermie returned from their ride, Leah's mom had a popcorn snack waiting for her.

"That smells so good!" Leah said and grabbed a handful. Hermie came down from Leah's shoulder and stole a kernel that had fallen on the floor. He took it into his paws and munched the kernel down. The kernel looked huge compared to Hermie's tiny paws. It took several minutes for him to eat the entire thing. He ate it from all angles as he turned it, and then took a bite.

When he was ready, he grabbed the next kernel, then ran off to the living room with it. Almost immediately, he was back, asking for another tasty treat.

"How did you eat that one so fast, Hermie?" Leah wondered. "Here you go." She handed him another kernel. He once again ran off with it, and came back immediately, ready for another.

"What is going on?" Leah asked. She bent down and gave him one more kernel, but this time she watched where he went. He ran to the living room with the popcorn, jumped up on the couch and hid it in the couch cushions. Leah called Kacy in.

"You have to see this!" She handed Hermie another kernel, and they all peeked into the living room to see where he went. Up the couch he went and stuffed the kernel into the sofa cushion. "He wants to save them up so he could have a snack later!" They laughed at his ingenuity. Leah's mom smiled as she dug the popcorn out of the cushions.

"Leah, we have to decide what to do with Hermie next week while we are gone," Leah's mom said. "Dad has a YMCA of the Rockies conference at the Estes Park Center, and we need to stay a couple of nights in the Alpen Inn lodge."

"Kacy can keep Hermie." Leah pleaded with her, knowing that Kacy was staying home on this trip.

"*No way*, I am *not* keeping Hermie. What if something happens to him while you are gone? I do *not* want that responsibility," Kacy said firmly. Leah's heart broke. What would she do with him? Where could he stay?

Leah's mom thought for a minute. "I guess we can take him with us," Leah's mom said with a smile.

"Yeah! Let's do it!" Leah said, relieved.

The drive over Trail Ridge Road was always stressful. Crossing high mountain peaks with extreme weather, sharp drop-offs, and hairpin turns made Leah carsick every time. This trip was doubly so. Leah didn't want Hermie to get sick from the motion or dehydrated from the elevation. The weather changed rapidly, but tucked in his borrowed gerbil cage, he stayed calm next to Leah. With the YMCA sign in full view, she felt relief that the harrowing drive was over.

The Admin Building was bustling with people, as usual, looking to get checked in. The old wood floor creaked with every step Leah took. *Good thing Hermie is in the cage and covered*, she thought. *He would not like all these people.* She made her way to the Rustic Room and got a vanilla ice cream cone with the coins in her pocket. *People would sure be surprised if they knew I had a squirrel in here*; she giggled to herself and made her way out to the balcony to wait for her mom. She enjoyed the view of the mountains and the alpine flowers.

"Here you go, little guy," Leah said as she broke a piece of her cone off and snuck it through the split in the blanket that covered the cage. In a few more minutes, Leah's mom emerged with the room keys.

"Let's get him settled," she said and made her way to the car.

The next morning, Leah got dressed for the Ladies' Meeting she was to attend with her mom. She smoothed her dress out and tied her hair up with a ribbon. It felt strange being so fancy, but she enjoyed dressing up for a change. Except for the dirt hidden deep in her rein finger, she cleaned up nicely. Leah filled Hermie's food and water dishes in the gerbil cage while Hermie ran free around the room.

"Hermie," she said. "It's time to go back in the cage." Hermie didn't make a sound. She waited for him to come running up her leg. Concerned, she turned to her mother who was getting ready in the bathroom. "Mom, have you seen Hermie? I don't see him anywhere."

"Let's look under all the furniture." Leah bent down and peeked under the bed. No sign of him. She looked under the desk and under the heat register…still no sign of him. "Did he get out of the room when we weren't looking?" Leah's voice shook. The last piece of furniture was the dresser, and she bent down to look under it. There she found Hermie, munching on a square of dark chocolate the same way he had eaten the oats.

"Hermie!" Leah yelled and picked him up. Her mom quickly grabbed the chocolate and threw it away, then looked him over. She held him close and stroked him softly.

"Leah," her mom said quietly. "Dark chocolate is poisonous to animals. Hermie may not make it out of this alive. He is the same size as a rodent and his body may not be able to handle it."

Leah screamed out in anger, "Why would he want to eat poison?" She held him next to her cheek and kissed him on his head. Teardrops fell on his back as Leah could not control her sadness.

"We have to go now," her mom said softly, putting her arm around Leah. "Let's give him some milk to drink. That may help him absorb the chocolate."

Leah put Hermie in his cage and stroked his back one last time.

The ladies' luncheon was filled with flowers, lace, and pretty colors. Finger sandwiches, punch, and desserts of every kind lined the tables. A speaker spoke about antique hats and showed her treasures. It was a nice talk, but all Leah wanted was to be back with Hermie.

I could be losing him right now, Leah thought, biting her cheeks, trying not to cry. Leah's mom noticed her expression and excused herself a few minutes early. They rushed back to the lodge in silence.

When Leah walked into the room, she found Hermie curled up, sleeping in his cage. He did not move. Was he dying? Was he in pain? Leah swallowed hard at what she might find. Cautiously, she opened the cage door, and without warning, Hermie jumped up, ran up her arm and snuggled in her hair.

"Ah, Hermie, you're okay!" Leah leaned in and snuggled with him, overjoyed that he was okay.

After a few weeks, Hermie reached adult size and seemed strong enough to survive on his own. Leah knew she had to make the hard decision to let him go back into the wild where he would be happier with his family and the other squirrels. Her heart broke thinking about not having him to love anymore, but she knew it was the right thing to do.

The next day after lunch, she took him back to the backyard.

"Bye, Hermie." She lovingly took him off her shoulder and put him in the grass near where she had found him. Immediately, he turned around, ran up her leg, and sat on her shoulder. She felt honored and loved. He wanted to be with her. But at the same time, she was upset with herself.

"Mom," Leah struggled to say, "did I ruin him for good by keeping him too long?" She turned to look at her through her tears. "Would he rather be safe in my room or on my shoulder than out in the wild where he belongs?" Leah's mom smiled and gave her a minute to answer her own question. With a huge lump in her throat, Leah tried again. She widened her eyes so she could see clearly through her tears. Leah kissed Hermie on the head and put him in the grass below.

"I love you," she said in a broken voice. This time, he ran across the yard and halfway up the closest pine tree. He turned and looked at her and spoke like squirrels do. She imagined him saying, "Thank you for rescuing me and taking care of me." Hermie turned and ran to the top branches of the tree, and in a couple of hops, he was moving about the treetops, free and wild again.

Leah never saw him again, although there were many happy squirrels where she lived, and she was sure Hermie was one of them.

Hummingbird Feed

Ingredients:

1 part white table sugar (cane sugar, as used in baking)
4 parts warm tap water to help dissolve the sugar
Bowl or glass
Spoon
Feeder with red base and perches

Directions:

1. In your bowl, combine the warm water and sugar.
2. Mix with the spoon until the sugar has dissolved.
3. Do not add red dye, as that can be harmful to the birds.
4. Fill your feeders. You can store leftovers in the refrigerator for up to two weeks.
5. Hummingbirds like to eat at dawn and dusk.
6. Change your nectar every two days in hot weather, and once a week in cooler weather. Usually, they go through nectar in 1 1/2 days, if you keep the feeders filled.

CHAPTER 7

WORMS, WILLOWS, AND THE ROLLER COASTER

From the sheep barn, Rudy drove the small tractor, hauling loads of sheep manure and straw to build up the worm beds. With each pothole he went over, bits of straw and manure sprinkled the ground. Collie ran circles around the tractor, barking and herding it. Slowly he drove, making his way down the slope. The beds looked like worms themselves that crossed the meadow below the sheep barn. The organic mixture made an enriching home, and when combined with the water from Pole Creek, produced a bounty of worms. During the summer, Rudy and Clara Belle sold them at the local fishing store in Tabernash.

Leah and Kacy followed Rudy past the sheep barn toward the valley below and the horse pasture. Leah smoothed her hair into a ponytail and fastened it with her favorite purple marble ponytail holder. Dandy's bridle hung off her shoulder.

Clara Belle sat on the ground at the edge of the bed with her legs folded beside her and waited for Rudy to bring the haul in. She wore a cowboy hat, pants, and a shirt that draped over her body. Her hands were the only things left uncovered. They were black from the dirt that stuck to her skin and accented deep, white wrinkles. Dirt was caked under her fingernails. The same fingers that massaged dough into wonderful rhubarb pie were now buried in manure-rich dirt and earthworms.

"Goin' ridin' today?" Clara Belle said with a grin as the girls walked by.

Leah shook her head, smiled, and paused to watch her work.

With her pitchfork, Clara Belle stabbed the bed and turned over a large section of dirt. Hundreds of worms wiggled in the dark, rich soil. One by one, she pulled the worms out of the dirt and put them in the waiting bucket. Midway through the pile, she stopped, dusted the excess dirt off her hand, and reached into her pocket. She took a small pebble out of her left pocket and moved it to her right pocket.

"Why do you have rocks, Clara Belle?" Leah asked, noticing her bulging pocket.

"Well, I move a rock every time I reach a hundred worms," she said. "That's how I keep count of the worms."

"That is a lot of worms! Can I try?" Leah asked, kneeling down beside her. Clara Belle thrust her pitchfork in the raised bed and turned over the dirt. Leah pulled a worm out of the dark soil and watched it wiggle in the palm of her hand. It felt slimy and tickled a little as it looked for soft dirt to hide in. She dumped it in the bucket and grabbed a handful out of the multitude left in the dirt. *One, two, three*, she counted as she put them in the bucket and stopped at ten.

"Whew! That is a lot of worms to count." Leah was happy to let Clara Belle continue digging.

"It is a nice day for a ride," Clara Belle said, looking over at the horse pasture. "The horses are so close to the gate. You don't have much of a walk to catch them."

"You're right! Kacy, let's go." Leah stood up and dusted her hands on her pants.

Dandy was getting a drink of water at the creek when Kacy slid the latch open. When she did, he raised his head and flicked his ears back and forth. Suddenly, he snorted, then twisted his neck and threw his head. He picked his front legs up in a half rear, turned, and ran out of the water. All of the horses took off together as a herd and headed across the pasture to the trees.

"That little turkey! I didn't want to take a long hike to get him today." She picked her way across the dry rocks that poked out of water and crossed the stream. Delicately she walked toward the horses with one arm hiding the bridle behind her back and the other hand extending a horse cookie forward. This time, Dandy stood still and let her catch him.

"How about a nice ride today, eh, boy?" Leah whispered. She slipped the bridle on him and looped the reins around his neck. His lips smacked as he gobbled up his horse cookie. She turned him to the side of the bank, backed up a couple of steps, and ran to jump on his back. Lying across the withers, she shimmied to get the rest of the way up.

"Watch out!" Kacy shrieked, but it was too late. Buck, Rudy's bossy buckskin, lunged for Dandy and thrust his teeth right toward Leah's head. Goosebumps rose on her arms and her spine tingled. She screamed. Dandy lunged to the left, but Buck followed him, ears back and teeth bared. She had no control over Dandy's movement and couldn't get Buck away.

"Don't fall off or you will get trampled!" Kacy screeched.

Dandy shook his head with his ears back, but Buck was the boss, and he lunged one more time at Dandy. This time with his mouth open. Leah felt his breath on her neck and screamed in terror as Buck moved in. With one swift motion, he bit her ponytail holder off. Leah's blonde hair fell around her face. She sat up in time to see Buck mouthing her holder and shaking his head back and forth trying to eat it. He spat it out in disgust and it fell to the ground. Her stomach turned and she felt lightheaded.

"Are you *okay?*" Kacy asked in amazement. "Buck always wants to be boss of the herd. You got too close to him."

"Yes, I'm fine, let's get out of here." Leah reined Dandy out of the "danger zone" around Buck and headed toward the gate. *Of course, it was my favorite ponytail holder,* Leah thought, sighing. She tried to cue Dandy, but Buck had left her shaking and her legs felt weak.

"Kacy, I don't feel like changing into hot, stiff jeans or lifting a heavy saddle. Why don't we forget the long ride we had planned today and just play?"

"Okay, since it is such a warm day, let's stay in shorts and ride bareback," she began. "Our first stop can be the pond, and of course, we'll do the roller coaster." Kacy got off Brandy to open the gate. She pulled her boots off and stuffed her socks in them. Leah pulled her boots off while going through the gate. She tossed them next to it and her socks went flying.

"Ah, much better." Leah began to relax as the breeze cooled the sweat between her toes. "Being in shorts with no shoes, on a bareback horse in the middle of the summer, is one of the best things in the world!"

The girls turned the horses through the creek, splashing as they went. Rudy and Clara Belle waved from the worm beds. Leah squeezed Dandy into a fluffy lope, making an up-and-down motion like a carousel horse.

They followed the irrigation ditch next to the worm beds out of the valley. Crisscrossing them a couple of times, the horses hopped over the beds. The old woodpile was full of squirrels and rabbits making it their home. The carcass of a dead sheep lay next to it, attacked by a vicious coyote last week. The stench was unbearable.

Flies made a low hum over it. With her hand holding her nose, Leah urged Dandy past it. Once on the road, she could breathe again.

The horses wove their way through the trees as they headed to the pond at the bottom of the hill. Kacy turned Brandy to walk through it. Brandy lowered her head and snorted at the belly-high water. She walked slowly, feeling the bottom for rocks. Leah followed behind, making sure the water wasn't too deep and the footing was good. Once across the other side, Kacy asked, "Are you ready?" Kacy wheeled Brandy around, kicked her heels, and pushed Brandy to lope through the water. When she was up the bank on the other side, Leah let Dandy go.

"Yaw!" Dandy sprang forward. "Oh, that tickles my tummy!" Leah said, wrapping her free arm around her stomach. In water, a trot became a fancy prancing step and a lope felt like jumping in cotton. Water sprayed everywhere under the horses' running hooves, soaking both girls.

Dandy stopped short of the bank and stood in the shallow water.

"Don't go too slow, or he'll roll," Kacy warned. About that time, Dandy started pawing the water. His entire body rocked back and forth and he struck the water with his front leg. He stopped briefly to switch legs, and then smelled the water. Without warning, his front legs buckled, and down he went. Leah jumped off, just clearing his hooves. She bent forward to keep hold of his reins and watch him closely. It was dangerous standing so close to a horse while rolling. If he rolled toward her, his hooves would hit her.

Displaced water washed up Leah's legs. Dandy enjoyed the cool water and took a moment to relax in it. Then, with a snort and a shake of his head, he put his two front legs out to get up. At that precise moment, Leah jumped on his back and grabbed his mane as he stretched to stand. With all her strength she held on, avoiding sliding off his back while he was in the sitting position.

"Whew, I made it!" Out of breath, Leah pushed him out of the water to avoid a second roll. That ended his water party, leaving him dripping in the dry, summer dirt. He shook the excess water off like a dog. The force of the shake sent Leah scrambling to stay on as she was flung from side to side on his back. She walked him over into the old stand of pine trees and lay back on his rump.

"Since we are all wet, let's practice our trick riding. Their wet backs will help us grip them better."

Leah sat up and pulled her feet up. With a rein in each hand, she pushed off his neck and slowly stood on Dandy's back. Just behind his withers, she gripped his back by rolling her toes into his skin. Once she had her balance, she clucked to him to walk forward. Standing on the back of a horse was like being in a boat in high waves.

"Let's see how far I can go before falling off," Leah said, holding her breath. "The first step is the hardest." Dandy took an awkward step forward, and Leah wiggled to stay balanced. "*One* step…*two* steps…" Leah buckled her knees and sat back down on Dandy's back. Kacy laughed.

"I wanted to avoid falling off," Leah said, as she flipped her leg over the withers, sat sideways momentarily, and then flipped the other leg over, riding backward instead.

"You'd better keep your legs off his flanks," Kacy warned, "otherwise, you'll send him bucking." Holding the reins in both hands, Leah worked to push her legs back, away from his flanks. The sitting position was very awkward for the horse and it was hard to convince him to walk forward. Dandy kept looking back at her, telling her it was wrong.

Abandoning the attempt, Leah turned herself around and pushed herself back on Dandy's hindquarters. Perched on his rump, she stretched her long, leather reins over his neck, withers, and back.

"Come on, you old plow horse," Leah said, slapping the reins on his back pretending he was pulling a wagon. Dandy looked around at her to see if she was serious. "That's right, walk on." Leah kissed to him. "Being on the hindquarters of a horse feels more like an elephant walking." She giggled and let him walk a couple of steps. "I wish I had my saddle on. I could lie across the saddle and put my legs straight up…at the canter," she said, smirking at the difficulty of the move.

"Better yet, you could pretend that you were a Cherokee Indian by hiding your entire body on only one side of the horse while holding onto the mane," Kacy said, one-upping her. "Indians used to do that to not be seen. They could hide by hanging on without the saddle and at a full gallop!" Leah raised an eyebrow in disbelief.

"Kacy, I'm starving, let's eat lunch," Leah said. "How 'bout by the tree over there?" She grabbed the bag of trail mix, dove her hand into it, and pulled out the candies, eating them first.

The horses welcomed the break. Under the long branches of an old pine tree, they lowered their heads and napped. The girls rotated around and faced backward, eating lunch on their horses' hindquarters.

"This is the perfect table," Kacy said running her arms over Dandy's hindquarters. "Here's your sandwich."

Leah munched down on her peanut butter and jelly sandwich, but before she could finish it, she lay down over Dandy's hindquarters. With her arms dangling down each side, the rest of her PBJ slipped out of her fingers. The sounds of the robins, chipmunks, and hummingbirds made an unlikely chorus. She heard the gentle flap of the camp robber's wings as he swooped in to pick up the treat she dropped. A light breeze waved the top branches and felt like massaging fingers over Leah's back, relaxing her into a light snooze.

Swoosh, Dandy's tail hit her in the face, stinging it intensely. She quickly sat up as he raised his hip and kicked at the monster horsefly that attacked his belly. The movement almost jolted her off his back. She was awake.

"Nice nap. Now let's go jump and do the roller coaster," Leah said, spinning forward, stretching her arms. Kacy rolled up from the "bed" she was lying on. Brandy was catching the last few winks when Leah turned Dandy back toward the Just Ranch.

"Hey, wait a minute," Kacy said, scrambling to turn around on Brandy. Midturn, perched sideways on Brandy, she took an awkward step, and Kacy almost fell off. All of her weight was on one side of Brandy's back. She tilted forward and swung her leg over and grabbed the reins.

The jumping ring was a figure-eight course built in a stand of old pine trees just outside the ranch gate. These pine trees were some of the largest and the oldest on the YMCA property because they once had avoided a forest fire that otherwise ravaged the countryside a hundred years earlier. The ring was made up of logs that had fallen naturally and others that had been strategically moved into place. Sticks lined the path around the jumps to mark the course. The jumps were small enough to be fun while dogging the trees, tree branches, and intersection in the course.

"Kacy, jump the three-log jump." It was the biggest jump out there, and Kacy sneered at the challenge. She turned Brandy around to give herself plenty of room. Brandy lunged forward as Kacy dug her heels in. With one huge effort she was over the logs, jumping far above what was required. Her long, curly brown hair lit up in the sunlight.

"Wow, that horse can jump!" Leah said, admiring the pair.

"Leah, you go first around the jumping ring." Kacy waited while Leah pushed Dandy over the first two jumps.

"Whee," Leah yelled. Running through the trees was exhilarating.

When Leah was a couple of jumps ahead, Kacy squeezed Brandy hard and she went into a lope from a standstill. She ducked and dodged tree branches while lining Brandy up perfectly for the jumps at fast lope. The single tree, multiple sticks, and branch jumps were all along the first loop of the figure eight.

From the corner of her eye, Leah saw Kacy coming full speed through the crossing of the middle of the 8.

"Watch out!" she screamed as Kacy pulled Brandy up, shifting her weight back and practically doing a sliding stop, narrowly missing trees and each other.

"That...was...close!" Leah said, struggling to get words out. Out of breath, she walked Dandy out of the ring.

"We'd better quit jumping while we are ahead."

When they made it back to the ranch, their legs ached and they were tired from hanging onto the back of a horse. The chickens scurried as the horses walked through them, heading down to the horse pasture. The mountains gave off a warm, friendly glow. Everything was painted in a pink hue. The air became crisp.

Kacy jumped off Brandy and opened the gate to the horse pasture. "I don't want to let them go yet. Hey, let's ride like cowboys chasing the herd through the willow bushes." Leah nodded her head in agreement.

Thick willow bushes followed Pole Creek. Sheep had carved a narrow trail through them that was barely visible from above. It was plenty of room for a sheep to pass through, but the trail was hidden as the branches fanned out.

"Let's go!" Kacy yelled. Dandy lowered his head and cantered through the path. He jumped back and forth to follow the trail and avoid the branches and the mud. It was difficult knowing what direction Dandy was going, because Leah could not see the trail. Willow branches whipped at her sides and snapped back after she passed. She struggled to stay balanced on him.

"It's hard to hang on, but so much fun!" Leah said, as Brandy made it through the last of the bushes.

"Yahoo!" Leah urged Dandy back down the same path. Finally, Leah pulled Dandy up on a grassy area next to the stream.

"That was fun," she said, "but we've been waiting all day for the roller coaster!"

The roller coaster was part of a hillside where soil had eroded, leaving banks which were set perfectly at a forty-five-degree angle as the valley floor rose to meet them. They were sloped so one had to run sideways, across the steep hillside. It was hard to sit up straight on a horse. Hitting the bank at an angle meant being pushed onto the horse's back, like the hard turn of a roller coaster; missing it meant you were off. All done at a lope, the roller coaster was thrilling.

"Keep him straight," Kacy reminded Leah. Leah nodded with a focused look of determination. She squeezed Dandy into the lope. The minute she hit the bank, Dandy followed the turn and forced Leah to hang on tight. *First loop, second loop.* Then he was out, on flat ground again. Leah pulled him up next to Kacy.

"What a blast! Leah screamed. "The force of the turns really does feel like a roller coaster."

"My turn," said Kacy. She moved the reins forward, and Brandy took off in a fast lope. As Kacy met the first hard turn, Brandy misstepped and popped out of the turn and above the bank. Her body twisted as she looked for solid footing. Kacy wrapped her legs around Brandy's barrel, hanging on for dear life. With one swift motion, Brandy lunged in midair, twisting into a rollback that put her back on the valley floor. Brandy stopped immediately, breathing deeply with a wide-eyed look. Kacy flew off Brandy's back and landed on her feet, like a professional rodeo cowboy.

"That was scary!" Kacy said. "Let's try this again, Brandy." She turned Brandy into the curve and jumped on her back. She walked to the beginning of the bank and kicked her into a slow lope. She did a circle before heading into the roller coaster. Brandy was much more alert and careful with her footing.

"*Yippee,*" she said as she rounded the turns and pulled up next to Leah.

"Look, Rudy is coming down with Collie to herd the sheep in for the night," Leah said, pointing to the top of the hill.

"Girls, do you want to help get the sheep in?" Rudy asked, sending Collie out to the far reaches of the pasture.

"Yes!" they both answered at the same time.

"They aren't cows, but sheep will do," Leah said, excited to do some work with Dandy. The girls turned the horses to the north end of the pasture. The sheep saw Rudy and headed up to the barn in a line at a slow, processional walk.

"No fair," Leah protested. "They know to go to the barn at this time of the day. When Rudy comes down to the pasture, they go to him! We can't herd them at all."

"I know," said Kacy. "Let's just follow them in." Leah let Dandy's reins out and he followed slowly behind the sheep, careful as to not spook them. Rudy closed the gate behind the remaining ewes.

"Thanks for your help." He waved. "You are good ranch hands," he said with a smile. Leah smiled and turned Dandy toward the horse pasture. She opened the gate, slipped the bridle off and reluctantly let him go. Dandy flicked his head as the bridle came off and bolted off toward the other horses. The rocks clanked as he ran through the creek. He acted as if a big bear was chasing him and he had to get away. Once near the other horses, he lowered his head to the ground and walked in a circle.

"He's going to do it…watch! He's going to do it," Kacy said. "And there he goes!" Dandy folded his front legs, then his back legs, and his massive hindquarter hit the ground.

"Bang!" Leah laughed. "The earth shakes." There wasn't really a sound, just a large animal rolling in the grass. Brandy followed suit a few feet away. Dandy finished rolling back and forth and stood up, shook his body, and started chewing, licking his lips, satisfied his work was done.

Leah and Kacy turned to walk to the grain bin, bridles hanging over their shoulders.

"Bye, Rudy, we'll see you tomorrow," Leah said, as they put the bridles away and began the walk home. Rudy waved from the corral with buckets in tow for feeding the lambs. Leah smiled at the fun she had had that day.

Mountain Trail Mix

Ingredients:

2 cups Rice Chex™ cereal
1 cup raisins
1 cup candy-coated chocolate
1 cup cocktail peanuts
1/2 cup chocolate chips

Directions:

Combine all ingredients and mix well. Store in airtight container.

CHAPTER 8

CLARA BELLE STARR

"Let's tie our bedroll and poncho onto the back of the saddle." Kacy grabbed a radish and turned to Rudy. "We'll head out to Leo Marte Lake and meet you there this afternoon."

"All right," Rudy said, pushing his glasses up. "We'll drive up the back way. Remember, don't cross over the McCurdy property," he warned. "Be sure to go up Blue Ridge Mountain to get there."

"Okay," they answered in unison.

The door creaked as the girls left the farmhouse to get the horses. Leah slid the latch to open the log gate. They walked down the hill, ran across the board that crossed the creek, then crawled through the strands of barbed wire. The horses were close by and easy to catch. They brought them up to the barn and saddled them with all their gear.

I don't know why we can't go through Mr. McCurdy's property, thought Leah. *Is it because the gate is too hard to open? Are there dangerous bogs? Or do bears live there?* The girls headed out of the ranch and up the trail to Leo Marte Lake. *Clip, clop, clip, clop* echoed off the trees as the road narrowed.

"Hey, let's stop at the Gold Mine first." Kacy pulled Penny up and tied her to a tree just outside the cave. She climbed up the bank. Leah followed closely behind as the cold air from the cave surrounded her. The air smelled musty and felt wet and heavy. Sounds of drips could be heard deep inside the cave. *What if there is an animal deep in the cave...or...a man.* Leah thought. They turned on their flashlights and headed in.

"The prospector was looking for gold and died trying to find it," Kacy whispered.

"Stop it, you're just trying to scare me!" Leah yelled.

Deeper and deeper they went into the mine. After just a few steps in, light could no longer be seen from the entrance. The mine got wetter, the rocks got bigger. It was harder to walk. Drops of water dribbled from the ceiling as it seeped through the mountain and hit the stones below.

The walls narrowed like the cave would absorb them into the mountain. Leah bent over to avoid hitting her head. It was black as night except for the small light cast from their flashlights. Finally, the mine came to an abrupt end and a wall stood before them. It felt like toil and frustration had left its mark. The miner just gave up. All the effort he put into the mine had yielded him nothing but heartache.

"This is where he stopped and died," Kacy said in a spooky voice that echoed off the walls. The air was suddenly colder.

"What if the vein of gold was one pick away?" Leah wondered. The girls were silent for a moment. The soul of the prospector could eerily be felt in the air. *Squeak, squeak, flap, flap, flap.* Leah screamed and dropped to the ground as a bat broke the silence in the cave. The ground was wet, and Leah's knees got soaked. Once the bat flew over, Leah jumped up and ran out of the cave. The rocks in the cave tripped her up and she went sailing forward, landing on a damp spot of gravel. She skidded on the rocks and scraped her hands.

"Are you okay?" Kacy said, pulling Leah up by her underarms.

"Yes, let's get out of here." She stumbled up and walked out the entrance of the cave and slid down the bank. The warm air released them from their tomb.

"Let's get to the lake," Leah demanded. She untied Dandy and swung her leg over the saddle. "That place is too scary."

Kacy led the way on Penny down the road.

"Hey, Kacy, what would happen if we went through Mr. McCurdy's place?" Leah asked. "No one would ever know, because Mr. McCurdy rarely comes over this way."

Kacy contemplated. "I don't know."

"It sure would be shorter and we wouldn't have to wind up Blue Ridge Mountain like the train up Rollins Pass. Leah held her breath and waited for Kacy's answer, hoping she would agree.

"Okay, let's try it," Kacy said.

"Yes!" Leah was relieved and excited. Kacy veered off the road to the trail and headed to the McCurdy place. Pine trees turned to aspen trees, which carpeted the rolling hills before them.

"Okay, here is where the trail ends," Kacy said, leaving the safety of the path and heading straight up the draw toward the mountain. The horses pulled their legs up high to get over the tall grass and hidden timber. Their backs rocked side to side. Kacy kept a safe distance behind, and concentrated on the route. Leah kept her eyes on the ground and leaned over and to help Dandy pick his path among the skunk cabbage, logs, and hidden holes.

Suddenly, Dandy stopped and threw his head up and put his ears forward. His head almost hit Leah's chin and she nearly went over his shoulder. She pushed herself up and braced for what she would see.

"Oh, I hope it's not a bear," Leah whispered as she scanned the scene. "Oh, no, it is much worse! The person I did NOT want to see." she gasped.

"It was Mr. McCurdy, the man who did not like trespassers on his property." He stood tall, armed with a silver axe in his hands and a mean scowl on his face. Leah was in shock and stared at him for what felt like an eternity. Her mouth was open and her eyes were wide. All she could hear was Penny breathing behind her. She swallowed hard.

"What are you girls doing here?" Mr. McCurdy asked in a gruff voice. His brown duck jacket was faded and torn. He pushed his hat up and glared at Leah. She pulled her reins through her fingers to shorten them. She would have to turn Dandy hard and gallop if things got ugly. She didn't want to do that because the terrain was so dangerous. He could fall in a hole, and then where'd she be? Besides, she'd have to run over Kacy to get away from him.

She stammered, "We…we are trying to get to Leo Marte Lake." Wide-eyed, she stared at him, trying to read his rage.

"I see." He spat his tobacco on the buck fence and swung his axe down with such force it split the log and made a loud noise. Leah jumped. She slowly pushed her heels down, and feathered her legs, to let Dandy know something was about to happen. He flicked his ears back and forth, waiting for her command.

He drew his arm up and pointed. "Come through the fence here and follow the draw up. You'll run right into it." Leah quietly let her breath out. She didn't want him to notice how afraid she had been. "You girls be careful, you hear?" Mr. McCurdy warned.

Her voice shook. "Thank you, Mr. McCurdy." She pushed Dandy into a fast walk forward through the spot in the fence where he said to go. With every step away from Mr. McCurdy, she felt safer. She waited until they were a good distance away and turned around to look at Kacy. Her eyes were as big as saucers.

"Can you believe that just happened?"

Kacy just shook her head but didn't speak a word.

The last part up of the trail was narrow and rocky. The horses struggled to step over the big rocks as they made their way to the lake. Finally, blue sky could be seen through the trees and the lake was in full view. The water was dark, reflecting the pine trees growing around it. The Chalk Cliffs hung over the lake at the far end. Kacy led the way to a wide spot next to the water's edge.

Leah got off Dandy but could barely walk. Her legs were sore and tired from the ride. She untied the lead rope from the saddle horn and pulled Dandy's bridle off and hung it on the saddle horn. His halter was already on, so she led him to the lake for a drink.

"Good boy, Dandy. That was a long ride, wasn't it?" Dandy drank the water. With each swallow his ears flickered forward, huge gulps traveled down the length of his neck, and the sockets above his eyes popped up. When he had his fill, he started chewing, letting the water drip from his mouth. Leah scratched behind his ears.

"Okay, boy. Let's go tie you up to a tree." She found a tree to tie him to and loosened his cinch. She unhooked her saddlebags and bedroll and put them next to the lake. Kacy did the same thing. Leah grabbed her water bottle out and took a drink. She looked out over the tree-lined lake. Across the black lake were dark shadows into the pine trees. The thick vegetation around the lake made her look twice for intruders.

"Kacy, I feel like something is watching us," Leah said, shaken from the day and getting an uneasy feeling.

"Well, you know there are mountain lions and bears up here, don't you?" Kacy said.

"Oh, be quiet." Leah didn't want to admit that she did. "What if Rudy and Clara Belle couldn't make it up? It is too late to go back down the mountain now, before it gets dark."

"We may have to stay here alone," Kacy said in a spooky voice.

Leah looked in every dark place for eyes looking back at her. Time stood still. There was no wind, no birds, no chipmunk noise; even the horses were quiet. A serene place that she should enjoy felt dark, tense, and uneasy. A twig snapped at the other end of the lake. Leah searched for the predator. An owl hooted in the darkness. Leah sat on a stump, convinced she would be overtaken by something. The hair on the back of her neck stood up. A bloodthirsty mosquito buzzed around her head. There was a splash in the lake at a distance.

Finally, she heard the faint sound of an engine. Rudy and Clara Belle *were* on their way. It was confirmed when Leah saw the red-orange truck making its way through the trees. She felt a huge sense of relief and ran over to greet them.

"Hi, girls, did it go okay?" Rudy asked, grabbing his lasso off the gun rack in his truck.

"Yes, it did," Leah looked at the ground and dragged her toe in the dirt.

"Over the mountain like I said?" Rudy asked.

"Well, uh, we went through Mr. McCurdy's place."

Rudy smirked. "I know. Mr. McCurdy called your dad."

Leah gasped.

"He asked for you not to use his property any longer," he said.

"We won't do it again, believe me."

"Well, all right, now help me get the horses tied to the picket line." Rudy gave Leah one end of the lasso. "Hold on to this end and I'll string it down to the other tree." Leah held on tight as Rudy walked away from her. It was hard to hold because he wanted the tension tight. He tied it with a half hitch on a tree, then came back to tie Leah's end.

"There now. You can unsaddle the horses." Rudy stood with his thumbs in his belt loops. "And tie them up to the rope. That way they can move a little."

Leah threaded the leather through the cinch and took the saddle off. She walked across the trail and laid it on a fallen tree.

"Oh, no," Clara Belle said, "that saddle is part of your bedroll, just like the cowboys." She motioned for her to put it in the camp.

Clara Belle lifted some rocks from the edge of the lake and made a circle near the bank. With her boot, she scraped out the small sticks and pine needles from the area.

"We'll have our campfire here." She pointed to the circle of rocks. "Bring your saddle and pad over." Leah lifted her saddle back up and walked over to the fire ring. Clara Belle lifted her saddle pad off and put it on the ground.

"Now, lay your saddle like this," she said, folding the fenders in and making a pillow with the saddle. "Grab your bedroll and lay it out." Leah grabbed her saddlebags and bedroll. "Let's just hope Belle Starr doesn't come by tonight and steal it!" She giggled at the mischief that outlaw caused. "Rudy, you get the fire going and I'll start supper."

Rudy grabbed logs out of the truck to build the fire, and Clara Belle got the large skillet. She sat on a tree stump and sliced the potatoes and onions. They fell into the cast-iron skillet on the ground as she sliced. Rudy strategically placed the logs in the fire ring, and with part of a newspaper, got the fire going. He then placed a grate over the logs for Clara Belle to cook over.

"Kacy, grab the other iron skillet from the truck." Clara Belle motioned to the pickup. "Be careful, it's full of biscuits." The potatoes sizzled over the fire. In the pot, Clara Belle warmed pinto beans. Smells from the dinner wafted above the fire, and Leah's stomach growled. She sat mesmerized by the flames and the sounds of the cooking food. She peeked under the lid on the biscuits. They had doubled in size and were golden brown.

"It looks like we are ready to eat," Clara Belle announced. "Leah, go grab us some plates." Leah jumped up and pulled the blue tin plates out of a box. She held them out for Clara Belle to fill. The plates warmed up quickly as the hot food was dished up. She sat down with hers and balanced it on her knees. *Yum.* The flakey biscuit melted in her mouth as she mopped up the pinto beans. The potatoes were browned on one side, just the way she liked them. The ride had made her hungry and she gobbled up the food.

The fire crackled. Leah finished her dinner and got up to check on the horses. Quietly, she untied Dandy and let him over to a log next to the fire. She hopped on, then put her head on his neck and laid her legs over his rump. He rested his leg and relaxed. "Tell us some more stories about Belle Starr," she said, peeking through his ears.

"You know, Clara Belle was named after the outlaw Belle Starr," Rudy started. "Her daddy knew the Starr clan from the Indian Territory. She was a crack shot just like Clara Belle."

Clara Belle giggled. "She used to ride sidesaddle, as most women did then, you see. She dressed in a black velvet riding coat, a top hat, and carried two pistols with a cartridge belt around her waist."

"Well, now, see this hat?" Rudy said taking his cowboy hat off. The hat was nothing to look at. It was well worn with dirt all over it. One side was bent up higher than the other one and it looked like it had been stepped on a time or two. He handed it to Kacy.

"Clara Belle, tell them where you got this hat."

"Well," Clara Belle lit up in the glow from the fire. "My daddy once hired a Cherokee Indian to work for him on the ranch named Joe Bailey. One day, Papa sent him to fix fence in the northern pasture. When he was in the middle of stretching the wire, Belle and Sam Starr snuck up on him." She looked around at Kacy and Leah. "Belle whispered, 'Stick 'em up!' Joe jumped straight up in a fright and dropped his hammer right on his toe. She laughed and slapped him on his back. He knew Belle and Sam from them riding into his camp from time to time. She would rope his bedroll and jerk it right out from under him.

"Belle said, 'Joe, I left an old hat down the fence row that I don't want anymore. Why don't you go get it? It might suit you.'" Clara Belle snickered and narrowed her eyes. "Well, later that day, Joe Bailey finally made it down the fence line. He found that hat sittin' on the post just like Belle said, only it was filled with gold coins from a bank they had just robbed." Leah gasped and sat up. "That's right," Clara Belle said. "They had just robbed a bank and didn't want to take the heavy coins with them."

"Wow," Kacy said. "This hat was in a robbery from the olden days!" Dust filled every crease. She ran her hand over it and flipped it on her head. "I feel just like an outlaw." Clara Belle chuckled.

"Okay, girls, let's put the horses up and get to bed." Rudy stood and grabbed the hobbles out of his truck. "It's okay, Dandy." He leaned over and buckled the leather straps around Dandy's ankles. Dandy snorted, but was more interested in finding a cookie in his pocket. Leah looked at him with concern.

"The hobble between his feet prevents him from going too far." Rudy unsnapped Dandy's lead rope, but left his halter on. "It's okay," Rudy said, knowing Leah's uneasiness. He did the same thing with Penny. "Now, let's hit the hay."

Rudy put another log on the fire and pulled the blankets out for the girls. Leah rested on her saddle pillow, which was surprisingly comfortable. She studied the bright stars, looking for the Big Dipper, and imagined outlaws looking at the same stars. The crisp air smelled fresh, and she took a deep breath. The fire crackled. The creek bubbled as it left the lake. The slight breeze gently waved the tops of the pine trees. The horses settled and the glow of the fire lulled her to sleep.

Suddenly, the chains were *clanking* and she was jolted awake. The horses were on the move. Her eyes opened to pitch black. Out of the darkness, a loud, blood-curling scream came from across the lake. It pierced the night and sent a shiver down Leah's spine. A mountain lion was on the prowl and unhappy that campers had invaded his home.

Rudy jumped up and grabbed the rifle he had lying beside him. Clara Belle stoked the fire and fed it to make a huge flame. Clara Belle's eyes told Leah to stay put. Her heart beat rapidly as she waited for Rudy. By the firelight, Leah saw Rudy lead Dandy back to the picket line and snap him back up to the lead rope. He quickly moved to get Penny and hooked her up too. He came and sat back down by the fire without saying a word.

Rudy kept his hand on the rifle as he sat. He looked around continuously, ready to defend the area if need be. Leah stared at the fire, heart pumping, and eyes wide open.

The next thing she knew, she awoke to the dawn. Clara Belle sliced bread for everyone while Rudy poured fresh coffee. Rhubarb compote was dropped on the slice. Leah smoothed it out with the back of her spoon and took a bite. The sweet sour taste woke her up for good. She licked her *slightly* dirty fingers and rose to tack up Dandy.

With the horses saddled, they packed up the bedrolls, tied on the saddlebags, and headed home. Rudy doused the fire with water, which caused a plume of smoke to go up. Clara Belle packed the last of the breakfast supplies. Leah rode down the bank from the lake, knowing the ride would be mostly downhill and uncomfortable. Dandy paused, not sure he wanted to step off the bank. Leah turned and waved goodbye to Rudy and Clara Belle, then squeezed her legs and urged him forward. Within moments, the lake disappeared behind them. The security of Rudy and Clara Belle were gone, and she once again faced the fear of seeing a mountain lion or bear. The trail wound its way through dark trees and rocky places that dotted the ridge.

"This is the way to Mr. McCurdy's property," Kacy said, pointing down the lush draw. "We'd better not go that way again." She turned Penny to the right. The trail led them into more trees.

"I don't like the switchbacks on this trail," Leah complained. "They make my legs tired." Just then, she felt a sprinkle hit her nose. "Oh, no, and now it is going to rain?" She turned in the saddle and untied her poncho. Reluctantly, she put it on and stretched it out so it covered her saddle horn in front and her bedroll in back. The girls made their way down to the bottom of Blue Ridge Mountain. The rain steadily increased.

"Now that we're on flat ground again, let's trot a little," Kacy yelled out. "The footing looks decent and not too slick from the rain." Leah nodded, and when she did, a stream of water poured off her cowboy hat. She was miserable and wanted to be off her horse, sipping hot chocolate in her pajamas at home.

"There's the Rowley place. We're making good time now," Leah said, excited to be so near the Just Ranch. As they rounded the corner and trotted past the old gold mine, Leah made out a familiar car coming up the road. Mud was flinging off its tires and the back end was sliding back and forth. The car stopped and her dad got out.

"Hi, girls," he said in a strained voice. "Are you doing okay?" By his tone, Leah knew something was wrong. She nodded her head and waited for him to continue. "I need your help." He held a radio next to his ear and took a minute to listen to the message. "A young boy named Freddie is lost and needs medication," he said sternly. "I need you to help in the search to find him. You two can go on horseback where we cannot." Leah's heart beat faster. She felt important. Her exhaustion and discomfort left her momentarily.

"Why don't you head over to the Rowley place and look in the meadow on the other side. I'll meet you there." Their dad jumped in the car and headed back down the road.

Leah turned Dandy back up the road to cross at the hideout, past the rhubarb patch and across to the Rowley homestead. The rain was coming down hard and she could barely keep her eyes open to see where she was going. They ran across the meadow and up the hill to the homestead. Leah felt like Belle Starr, running from the law. She noticed something black near a tree. *Please, don't be a bear*, she thought, and made her way over to it. It was a black leather jacket that was wadded up. The grass around it was matted down.

"It looks like someone slept here last night."

"We'd better tell Dad," Kacy said as she spun Penny around and headed past the homestead to the road. Their dad pulled up just in time. They told him about the jacket and took him over to see it. Within an instant of him radioing the news, several search cars came, including the sheriff, who got out of the car and barked orders.

"You girls go on horseback, check out the meadow toward the mountains and make sure he is not there." Leah didn't let him finish. She reined Dandy around and loped toward the meadow. Some old outbuildings of the Rowley homestead were on the left and Kacy decided to examine them first.

"Hey, let's go check out Outlaw Pass," Leah said, wanting to keep moving. "It's just over the hill."

"But, we're supposed to go down the meadow," Kacy said in protest.

"This will just take a minute, and we know where it is," Leah insisted, kicking Dandy off the trail.

As the girls made their way up the small hill through the trees, Leah thought about how miserable she was. Her jeans were completely wet, sticking to her legs. Her hands were wet from holding the reins, and the oil from the reins was coating them. *Just like Belle Starr, I have no choice but to stay in the saddle and tough it out.* Leah remembered the tracking skills of the Cherokee Indians, and looked for any more clues of the missing boy. He must be miserable too, she thought.

Rain dripped from Dandy's eyelashes and his mane streamed water from his neck. Leah looked down to drain her hat once more of the water. When she looked up again, she saw him. A small boy shaking from the cold sat next to a tree.

"There he is," Leah shouted, and in one swift movement kicked her legs out of the stirrups and hit the ground. Her stiff, wet jeans made it hard to walk.

"Hello, Freddie, you're okay now." The boy looked up at her with his big eyes, trying not to cry. "I'm going to take you home. Leah grabbed his hand and lifted him up to the front of the saddle. With all her strength, she pulled herself up behind, feeling the extra weight of the wet clothes. She wrapped her arms around the boy and grabbed the reins and started down the hill to the Rowley homestead.

"I hope Dad is still there," she said. Dandy seemed to walk more slowly, careful not to upset his additional passenger. They went a short distance and could see the outline of the cars parked at the Homestead. Kacy kicked Penny into the lope and waved her arms.

"Dad, we found him," she yelled. He ran toward them while talking in his radio. The camp EMT was with him and quickly pulled the boy off Dandy and wrapped him in a blanket. The sheriff whisked him away to be reunited with his family.

"Well, you girls are heroes," their dad said, standing in his jeans, mud boots, and camp jacket. "Everyone is grateful, and you did a great job." He smiled at them, his eyes filled with tears. "I am so proud of you," he said. "Make your way back to the Just Ranch and I'll pick you up so you won't have to walk home in the rain."

By the time they made it back to the Ranch, Leah's legs ached so bad she could hardly walk. In a chaotic manner, she pulled the saddle off with all the gear still on, and left it in the horse barn to dry. *I'll be back tomorrow to straighten this mess out*, she thought and went to take Dandy back to the horse pasture. Pink alpenglow settled on the mountains. A thistle patch caught Dandy's attention, and Leah let him have one more treat before she put him up. It was a delicacy for him. He loved the purple flower of a thistle. Carefully, he positioned his lips around it as to not stick himself on the sharp thorns, and then with one swift bite, he devoured it.

"It may not be gold coins, but is treasure to you." Leah stroked his rain-soaked neck and slipped his halter off.

Bucking Bronco
By Belle Starr

My love is a rider, wild broncos he breaks,
Though he's promised to quit it, just for my sake.
He ties up one foot, the saddle puts on,
With a swing and a jump, he is mounted and gone.
The first time I met him, 'twas early one spring,
Riding a bronco, a high-headed thing.
He tipped me a wink as he gaily did go,
For he wished me to look at his bucking bronco.
The next time I saw him, 'twas late in the fall,
Swinging the girls at Tomlinson's ball:
He laughed and he talked as we danced to and fro,—
He made me some presents, among them a ring;
The return that I made him was a far better thing;
'Twas a young maiden's heart, I'd have you all know;
He'd won it by riding his bucking bronco.
Now, all you young maidens, where'er you reside,
Beware of the cowboy who swings the rawhide,
He'll court you and pet you and leave you and go
In the spring up the trail on his bucking bronco.

CAMPFIRE BISCUITS

Pack dry biscuit mix in a plastic bag before you leave on your trip. Also be sure you have plenty of clean water, a mixing bowl and spoon, a skillet or a knife for whittling sticks.

Prepare a hot bed of campfire coals.

Mix 2 cups of biscuit mix with approximately 2/3 cup of water in the mixing bowl. The dough should be stiff and easy to handle.

Pat balls of dough into rounds of dough about 1/2-inch thick and 2 to 3 inches in diameter.

Place rounds onto a lightly greased skillet.

Place the skillet on the campfire grill and allow biscuits to bake uncovered until done.

Alternative:

Gather branches roughly 1 inch in diameter. Wrap the ends of each stick in foil and then stretch dough around the foil, roughly 3 inches long and 2 inches thick. Toast the biscuits over the bed of coals until golden brown. Slip off the branches and fill the cavity with your favorite filling.

CHAPTER 9

MIDDLE PARK FAIR

Dirt and feathers filled the air, as did the smell of chicken manure that lined the floor, a foot thick. The two-story chicken coup was so dusty, it was hard to breathe. Leah loved doing chores with Rudy, but collecting eggs was one of her least favorite. The stairs to the loft were rickety at best. Chicken boxes lined the walls at a height that was above her head, making it impossible to see what she was reaching into.

"You gather the eggs upstairs, and I'll get them from down here," Rudy said, ducking his head as a frantic, flapping chicken flew over it. Leah turned, and step by step, carefully inched her way up the stairs. She knew that Rudy walked up the stairs every day, but couldn't help the feeling of falling through the boards. The gaps in between the steps showed the chickens below. The first box was at the top of the stairs, and she reached into it.

"Sorry, old girl. I'm coming for your egg." Leah gently put her hand up to the box. The white hen sat there. The box was filled with straw, making the perfect nest. Leah reached in between her prehistoric, dinosaur-like chicken legs and wrapped her fingers around a smooth, warm egg. Slowly, she pulled the egg out. The chicken gave a halfhearted *cluck*, and went on ignoring her. Leah breathed a sigh of relief. She went on to the next chicken. The Plymouth Rock hen looked more zebra than chicken. Her black and white stripes waved as her feathers moved. Leah pushed her hand underneath. The hen head turned back and forth wildly. As Leah took the egg, she pecked wildly at her arm.

"Stop that!" she said, grabbed the egg, and jerked her arm out. "That was not very nice," Leah scolded her. Cautiously, she moved down the row to the White Rock, Shaver Red, and beautiful Buckeye, wanting to be finished with her chore.

"You are the last one," she said, and carefully put her hand under the Buckeye hen. The egg was warm as usual, but included a wet, squishy substance.

"Yuk." Leah pulled out the egg that was crowned with chicken poop smeared on one end. *Ewww.* She put her last one in the bucket. *I'm not eating that one,* she thought, and headed back down the stairs.

"Oh, good, you're done," Rudy said, just finishing the last nest. The downstairs had three times as many boxes as upstairs. "Let's go fry these up."

Rudy and Leah walked into the farmhouse with a bounty of eggs, and Clara Belle was ready.

"Put those eggs on the table," she said, smiling at Leah. Clara Belle sat down in front of the eggs. She took one in her hand and wiped it with a cloth. Then she put it on top of a can. The old coffee can had a hole cut out of the top of it and a light bulb inside.

"Plug this in, Rudy," she said, handing him the cord. The light in the can popped on, and in an instant, everything in the egg could be seen. She turned the egg over the light, inspecting every corner of it, looking for blood spots and other impurities.

"This one is perfect, why don't you get the fire going, Rudy, and we'll have some breakfast." Clara Belle handed him the egg, and he set it next to the wood-cooking stove. She continued to inspect the bucket of mostly brown eggs. The white, small, greenish eggs usually had fewer spots than the brown ones.

"We'll feed this one to the dog," Clara Belle announced and put the egg to the side. She grabbed another one and wiped it down.

"Leah, what are you planning today?" Rudy asked, putting a log into the firebox of the stove.

"I need to work Dandy. County Fair is coming up and I have to get him ready," Leah said, watching to make sure Clara Belle didn't miss anything.

Clara Belle giggled. "Used to be that when you wanted to train a horse, you rode him. Not to train him, but out of necessity. You had to get somewhere. The horse had to tie well, side-pass to open the gates, and get along with other horses.

"I remember one time," Clara Belle continued, "Rudy rode his horse to the neighbor's ranch for a visit. He tied his horse to the hitching post and went inside. When he came out, there was nothing left but the bridle, still tied to the post. That horse had rubbed the bridle clean off."

"Yes, and I had a long walk home." Rudy chuckled and adjusted his glasses. He cracked the egg open and dropped it into a cast-iron skillet; it splashed in an inch of bacon grease. The fire crackled as he lifted the top and put another log into the wood-cooking stove. The egg was done in an instant, and Rudy slid it on an orange plate for Leah.

"Yum," she said, "there really isn't anything better than a farm fresh egg." She mopped her plate clean with a piece of bread.

"Leah, why don't you get Dandy and I'll meet you in the lower pasture," Rudy said, sipping his coffee. "I'd like to see you work him."

"Great, I'll meet you there in a few minutes." Leah jumped up from the table, hugged Clara Belle, and ran out the door.

On her days off from the livery stable, Leah enjoyed summer rides. The weather was perfect and those were the days she had waited for all year long. She plucked Dandy out of the trees and headed to the barn to put her saddle on, working quickly before Rudy got busy with another chore. She rode him down to the lower pasture.

"Okay now, let's see you do a circle," Rudy said, standing with his thumbs in his belt loops and Collie at his feet. Leah kicked Dandy into a lope and started to do a circle. Dandy lunged a couple of strides, and then shook his head in protest.

"Give a light squeeze, not a kick, keep your hands quiet, and give him a leg to bend around," Rudy said. "The circle needs to be a circle, not a chicken egg, and very rhythmic."

Leah started Dandy again. This time, she gently squeezed her legs with the outside leg back to get the correct lead. She put pressure on her inside leg and asked him to bend in the circle. Next, she held her hands quietly, careful to not interfere with the bit in his mouth. She watched where she was going, a perfect circle, not a chicken egg. His strides were soft, round, and steady.

"That's it," Rudy commented, turning to head up to the barn. "Now do that again and again until it becomes second nature for both you and him."

Leah clucked softly to Dandy and pushed him back into a canter. She made kissing noises to him to keep his energy up. Around and around she went, riding circles in the pasture, remembering what Rudy once said: "Circles are the foundation of training." While cantering in the circle, she briefly trotted to change leads, and with that, changed direction into another circle. Over and over, she practiced this sequence until Dandy made a "flying" lead change in midair.

"Whoa, boy. Let's take a break." Leah dismounted Dandy and walked to the edge of the tree-lined meadow. With Dandy following, she dragged a fallen log out to the meadow, then she found some small pieces of wood to use as cones and put them in a line.

"There, now our Western Riding pattern is complete. Let's try it, Dandy." She mounted, then flexed him both directions to loosen up. She turned him through the imaginary arena gate and started the pattern. Walk to the pole, trot to the center, then canter through the cones, changing leads every time. She finished by stopping him and backing him up. She leaned forward and hugged him around the neck. "You did a good job, Dandy."

Leah headed back to the Just Ranch. Dandy was tired, and walked calmly. Leah took him to the horse barn and unsaddled him. She grabbed his halter and traded it for the bridle he was wearing.

"I know you are ready for dinner, but we need to work on showmanship first." Leah slipped the halter on. "We have been working on it for weeks, I know, but we have to be well trained for the judge." With Dandy in his halter, Leah walked up and down the road. "*Cluck*, come on, boy, let's go." Leah led him intently. He watched her every move and responded to every request. She walked forward briskly. He walked forward. She stopped. He stopped. She turned into him to do a pivot. He crossed his front legs and spun around on his hind leg.

"Oops, your front leg is back. Let's bring it together." She explained, "All four legs need to be square." Back and forth she worked with him until he understood his job. She trotted him forward, looking straight ahead, then stopped. She jiggled the chain, and he pulled his front leg back and set up. Rudy came out to "judge" her. He walked around Dandy, examining him, while Leah switched sides to professionally show her animal.

"Make it snappy," he said. "Move quickly or you'll find yourself in the same square as the judge." Rudy stroked Dandy's neck. "Good job working him. *Now* he knows showmanship."

"Thanks, Rudy," she said. "I have to take him home with me today. County Fair is tomorrow and I have to bathe him and leave early in the morning."

"All right. Thanks for telling me." Rudy turned and walked toward the grain bin to start his chores. Leah threw the bridle back on and headed home to put Dandy in the small corral that stood outside her home. Her dad had built it around a cluster of pine trees for lunch breaks and overnights.

"Okay, boy, are you ready for your show grooming?" Leah led Dandy over to the porch and plugged in her clippers. "We have to trim your whiskers off, after all." She turned the clippers on and gently ran them around his muzzle. His lips twitched from the vibration.

"It tickles, doesn't it?" She finished trimming his ears, bridle path, and feet. Leah pulled the hose from the yard and hosed him down. She squirted shampoo the entire length of his body on one side and worked it in with a plastic brush. It lathered into white foam that dropped off his back in globs. She repeated the procedure on the other side.

"Almost done, just a quick rinse, and conditioner in your tail." Leah rinsed him off, careful to get all of the soap out of his hair. A white puddle formed under his legs.

"Now," she said, "you are a beautiful show horse!" After he was dry, she put his cotton blanket on and wrapped his legs so he'd remain clean throughout the night. She wrapped his tail to keep the hair down and then put him into the corral.

"Thank goodness *he* is done," Leah sighed in relief. "But, I still have so much to do." Leah worked until bedtime cleaning and organizing her groom kit. The groom kit was an old popcorn tin with the three-way divider still inside. She filled one section with her brushes. The night before she had scrubbed them and laid them out to dry. Next she put the fly spray, baby oil, and Show Sheen in one third, and then she put her wraps and rags in the last section. Her clothes were next, and she buttoned the shirts up nicely and put them on hangers. Her chaps went on a metal hanger because they were so heavy. When everything was finished, she fell into bed.

"Get up, Leah." Her mom opened the door and turned her light on in what felt like a few minutes of sleep. "I let you sleep a little longer, but we've got to be on the road by six." Leah flew out of bed.

"Mom, why'd you let me sleep so long?" she snapped, not waiting for an answer. In an organized dance, she put everything on that she had laid out the night before.

"Ready, Mom," she said, passing her out the front door and down the porch stairs to get Dandy.

Neigh, Dandy whinnied. "I'm getting your hay, boy." Leah grabbed a flake that was next to the trailer and put it in the manger. She opened the doors to the horse trailer. Dandy's head was over the corral gate as he waited for Leah. She put his halter on and slid the pole gate open. With the straight load trailer open, she tossed the lead rope over his back and kissed to him. He loaded into the trailer.

"It looks like you didn't get too dirty last night," she said as she tied him at the manger and closed the doors. Everything else was loaded and she was ready to head to the show.

The dust swirled around the trailer as Leah's mom pulled into the fairground's parking lot. A banner over the gate read MIDDLE PARK FAIR, KREMMLING, COLORADO. She chose a spot next to the other trailers and got set to unload.

Neigh, Dandy protested in a strong tone. He was ready to get out of the trailer. She untied him from the front, and backed him out. He snorted, looked around, and raised his tail, trying to find some familiarity.

"You feel like a rocket, ready to blast off." She stroked his neck. "It's okay, boy. You can relax now."

Leah led him over to the row of stalls, which were buzzing with activity. She walked down the row until she found the stall door with her name on it and led Dandy into it.

"I'll be right back with your food and water." Leah latched the gate and walked back to the trailer. Dandy's hay net had a flake of grass hay in it. "This should tide him over," she said and carried an empty water bucket in the other hand. Once at the stall, she hung the hay net on the wall and searched for the water spigot. She found it two stalls down and filled the bucket full of water. She could barely walk and carry the heavy bucket too. The water sloshed from one side to the other, dumping about a third of its contents. She placed it next to the stall door.

Leah's mom called her for breakfast. She stepped into the truck camper and saw a familiar sight: Rudy's eggs. Her mom fried them up in the skillet along with toast and a side of Clara Belle's rhubarb compote. They tasted so good. She finished the last of the rhubarb up and went to get Dandy.

Leah slipped her halter on and pulled Dandy out of the stall. Silver lined the leather halter and sparkled in the sun. She wiped his body down one more time with a clean rag and sprayed him to make him shine. Next, she wiped his nose and brushed out his mane. The loudspeaker announced the start of the showmanship class, and Leah kissed Dandy on his freshly shaven muzzle.

"Good luck, Leah." Her mom smiled. "Remember, if the judge pulls you out of the line as an example, you've won the class."

Leah smirked in disbelief. "This is a huge class." She waited behind a beautiful bay named Rebel, and followed him in.

"Here we go, boy," she said and led Dandy to the gate. The judge was in the middle of the arena with a black cowboy hat on and holding a clipboard. He wore a coat and tie with jeans. *He looks serious*, she thought, and swallowed hard. He nodded to her to begin. Leah clucked to Dandy, who walked to the cone. She stopped him and set him up. The judge nodded again. The pattern was simple. Trot to the first cone, halt, pivot, walk to second cone and halt, back up. Contestant after contestant did the pattern while Leah and Dandy waited for the judge to begin his inspections.

"Don't fall asleep, boy," she whispered.

The judge walked from his position at the cone to the lineup of horses. He looked at each horse.

I'm glad I'm not first, she thought, trying to control her nerves, which got worse with every step the judge took closer to her. Finally, he nodded to her. With a small jiggle of the lead rope, Leah led Dandy straight for the judge and set him up. His feet were completely square. The judge walked around Dandy. He felt for any shavings stuck in his hair under his belly to confirm he was clean. He came back up to Leah and nodded to her. Quickly, she pivoted Dandy around and trotted back through the line, where she turned to face the judge one more time. The judge smiled in appreciation and moved down to the next horse.

"Whew, glad that's over, boy." Leah sighed. "Now we just have to wait for the placing."

The judge finished the inspections and met the ring steward in the middle of the arena. Leah watched the judge walking toward her end of the line. With a sharp turn of his body, he pointed to her and asked her to come out of the line. Her excitement was almost more than she could contain. She walked toward him and set Dandy up again, waiting for his nod. He tipped his hat, and she spun Dandy around for one more setup, then trotted back to the line.

The judge turned to the crowd. "Notice how this competitor lines her horse up and quickly turns him around." He turned and winked at her. "She did a great job!" The ring steward took over the microphone and announced, "First place goes to number hundred eighty-nine, Leah and Dandy Boy." Leah led Dandy over to the gate. The Middle Park Fair Queen had long brown curly hair and a crown on her cowboy hat. She handed Leah a blue ribbon with a large rosette and a trophy with a bronze horse on top of it.

Leah led Dandy back to the stall, shaking in disbelief. She slipped his show halter off and let him relax. "Good boy, Dandy, all the long hours of training finally paid off. I'm proud of you." She patted his muzzle and kissed it. "We have a little time now before the next class starts, so rest up. The performance classes are this afternoon."

The fairgrounds were busy with people working on their own animals. Leah laughed to herself, and thought it looked like an anthill. People were moving in all directions: some with buckets, some with rakes, some with feed. One boy was tugging on his steer, trying to get him to the wash rack. The sixty-pound boy was no match for the one-thousand-pound steer. Leah walked through the small animal barn. The air was thick with shavings smell from the chickens, turkeys, and rabbits that sat in metal cages. From one chicken cage hung a large ribbon. It had a purple rosette with lighter purple ribbons that hung from each side.

4-H Grand Champion—Poultry Division, the card said. It was the most beautiful chicken Leah had seen. The tan, black, and white feathers lay perfectly against her large chest.

"Boy, I bet Rudy and Clara Belle would like this chicken in their hen house," Leah remarked to herself. "She probably lays beautiful eggs."

A loud squeal caught her attention from the barn next door. A boy was trying to get his hog into the correct pen. The hog had other ideas, and two more boys jumped in to help. One used a cane and tapped his shoulders and hindquarters, trying to get it turned around. The other one had a square door and plopped it in front of the hog to prevent him from moving forward. The third boy poured feed into the pan, and that was what convinced him to finally go in.

The last exhibits to see were the "stills." Artwork, needlepoint, and decorated mailboxes lined the walls of the room. Canned goods sat on tables in the middle. Leah went over and examined the strawberry jam.

It is beautiful and looks really good, but I couldn't be inside that long to make it. I'd miss riding too much, she thought.

Leah walked out of the building toward the grandstand to get lemonade from the stand nearby. She saw a familiar sight which made her slightly uneasy. There, in front of the grandstand, sitting with a bunch of important people, were Rudy and Clara Belle.

"What are they doing here?" She waved to get their attention just as the announcer started talking.

"Ladies and gentlemen. It is my pleasure to announce Rudy and Clara Belle Just. They have been named 'Pioneers of the Year' for their work in settling the West. The Justs have been ranching in Grand County since the late eighteen-hundreds." The announcer handed a plaque to Rudy, who had his usual red-checkered shirt, jeans, and cowboy hat on. Clara Belle smiled proudly and her eyes sparkled as they peeked out from under her black cowboy hat. Leah clapped with everyone else and waited for the crowd to dissipate. *Rudy looks as uncomfortable as a horse jumping off a diving board*, Leah thought. He thanked his well-wishers and ducked to the side to see her.

"Wow, congratulations on your award." Leah gave Rudy a big hug. "What an honor to be recognized for lifelong work." She hugged Clara Belle as she walked up. "Can you come watch me ride?"

"Sure, we can!" Rudy seemed anxious to leave the award stuff behind. "How is Dandy doing today?"

"Great! We just won showmanship!" Leah led them to their seats next to the arena and ran to get Dandy out of his stall and ready for her riding events.

"Okay, boy, the fun events are next—Western riding pattern and reining." Leah wiped Dandy down and saddled him up. She wiped his muzzle and cleaned the dust that had just accumulated off her saddle.

The arena crew took a few minutes to set up the Western riding pattern.

"Cones and a painted rail look better than the sticks I was using, eh, Dandy?" She bent down and patted his neck. "We are fourth to go in the lineup."

When her number was called, she turned Dandy to side-pass to the gate. She opened the gate, walked through it, closed it, and side-passed away from it. To her surprise, there was wild applause for that attention to detail. She continued over the pole and her jog to the first cone. *Cluck*, she said under her breath. Smoothly, Dandy moved into the canter just like she had practiced. Leah queued him for his lead changes in the center of the figure eight, and Dandy changed leads precisely. It warmed her heart to know that Rudy was watching them. She finished the pattern by backing up. *One, two, three, four* steps. No more, no less; he did it perfectly. She walked out of the arena, and over to Clara Belle, who was leaning on the fence.

"The next class is class number sixteen, Senior Reining," the announcer said.

"Now, this is *my* favorite class," Leah said to Clara Belle. "Nothing is better than riding like cowboys do."

"Oh, yes," said Clara Belle. "Reining is a western event based on cowboys working cattle. The difficulty is in the sliding stops and rollbacks."

"I am doing pattern six today: one slow circle, one fast circle both directions, a sliding stop and a rollback." Leah waved to Clara Belle and waited by the gate. Her number was next.

The ring steward motioned for them to enter the arena. Leah stopped Dandy to settle him just inside the gate. She looked at the judge. He nodded. She moved her outside leg back, and Dandy started out in the left lead. His canter was so smooth. She noticed his orange mane ripple as his head went up and down. One circle slow, one circle fast, and she drove him into the sliding stop. Without delay, he did a rollback one hundred-eighty degrees, and she turned to do her next small circle slow, large circle fast, and she started her line for the sliding stop. Her leg flinched slightly and Dandy anticipated her stop.

"Oh no! We just lost some points. It's okay, Dandy, we can't worry about that now." With all of her strength, she drove Dandy to the end of the arena and laid out an impressive sliding stop. He rolled back and headed to the center of the arena, two pivots, and she was finished. The judge excused her from the arena.

Her mom met her at the gate. "Wow, Leah, that was a beautiful sliding stop."

"He hesitated on the first one because I wasn't driving him hard enough," Leah said, disappointed that she might have cost him the blue ribbon. She wanted to do the best in her favorite class.

"That was a *superb* ride," Leah's mom reassured her. "You might be surprised. The entire run looked great to me."

Leah knew her mom was trying to make her feel better, but she really felt like she let Dandy down. Waiting for the rest of the riders to finish felt like an eternity. The judge wrote his notes on a piece of paper and handed them to the ring steward who took them to the announcer's booth.

"Ladies and gentlemen, the judge has made his decision." The announcer paused to read his note. "Our first place rider is number hundred eighty-nine, Leah and Dandy Boy."

Leah sat on Dandy, not believing her ears, until she saw her mom, who looked at her with a big smile.

"Go get your trophy," said Clara Belle, who had made her way over to the gate. Leah rode Dandy over to collect her blue ribbon and trophy.

"That's the way to do it!" Rudy said. "And you too, Dandy." He opened his shirt pocket and pulled out a horse cookie.

Leah laughed. "No matter where you are, Rudy, you are always caring for animals."

Leah's mind swirled from the excitement of the day, but suddenly felt exhausted and longed for the peace of the ranch.

"Rudy, can I help you gather eggs tomorrow?" Leah said, handing her trophy to her mom.

"Why, sure, and we'll clear the stream, too." Rudy waved and escorted Clara Belle back to their pickup.

Leah took Dandy back to the stall where it was quiet and still. She rubbed his blaze and looked into his big brown eyes.

"I love you, Dandy. We make a great team." She hugged his neck and took in a deep breath. *Horses smell like nothing else in the world,* she thought. *They make me so happy.*

Leah turned to ready the horse trailer for the trip home. *Clank, ring, clank, ring,* her spurs went as she walked. She smiled. "Wearing spurs makes me feel like a true horsewoman, just like Clara Belle."

HORSE SHOW MOM
BY PATRICE LYNETTE ENGLE

We leave at six,
Breathe the cold brisk air,
We get them loaded,
And the day starts out fair.
The show grounds are crowded,
People are everywhere.
We are nervous as a cat,
But she doesn't express despair.
Our classes start,
The horses are groomed to shine
But when we don't win a ribbon,
She helps us not to whine.
And when the show is over,
The day is finally gone.
There will always be a place in our hearts,
For our horse show mom.

Rhubarb Compote

Ingredients:

3/4 pound rhubarb, cubed (about 3 to 4 cups)
3/4 cup granulated sugar

Directions:

1. In a saucepan, combine rhubarb with sugar over low heat. Cook about 5 minutes. When the rhubarb starts to soften, but before it falls apart, use a slotted spoon to transfer it to a storage bowl.
2. Continue to cook down the remaining liquid until it thickens, about 5 minutes longer.
3. Add the syrup to the bowl with the rhubarb, stir, and let cool. Compote will keep for at least a week in the fridge.

Enjoy over biscuits, toast, or yogurt.

CHAPTER 10

CHANGING SEASONS

Leah stood outside the ranch house, took a deep breath in, and looked across the hay meadows. The aspen trees behind her lifted and moved slightly in the whisper of a breeze. The fall season brought on a whole new set of sights and smells at the Just ranch. The air was crisp and filled with the smell of firewood and cinnamon. A calm fell over the Pole Creek Valley. There was less activity as tourists headed back home and kids headed back to school. The sunlight was golden, as were the aspen trees that dotted the property. Their luminous leaves lit up the dark evergreens like a painted canvas. Some years they were more golden, other years more red, and according to Rudy, it was because of the amount of moisture the "Quakies" received.

As the days shortened, the horses got restless and started to roam. They tiptoed through the barbed wire and set out to explore the entire YMCA camp, ending up near the Admin Building and Leah's front yard. The fences that held them before no longer did. They always stayed out of trouble, and got back home before anyone missed them. Buck was the only one left behind. He could stay in the pasture with a simple piece of barbed wire on the ground and not cross it. As tough as he was, he was afraid to cross barbed wire.

"Come on in, honey, and help me make an apple pie," Clara Belle called out from the screen door. She hugged Leah and handed her an apple as she walked in. "Let's get this peeled and ready to go in the pie." The peeler looked like a strange contraption mounted on the side of her wood block.

"Put the apple on the end and turn it." Leah did what was requested and slid the bottom of the apple onto the three prongs that held it, the blade resting next to the apple. She turned the crank. Red apple peeling came off in a long single piece. Once she reached the end of the apple, the peeling fell into the chicken feed bucket below.

"It worked! Here you go, Clara Belle." Leah handed her the apple.

"Good, now let's get this cut up for the pie." She sliced the apple into a bowl with cinnamon and sugar, and then continued working the pie dough with the rolling pin. She lifted it up on one end with the roller, and gently laid it over the pie plate. Leah poured the apple mixture into the pie plate, and watched as the second layer of crust went over on top. Clara Belle carefully pinched the ends, making an artistic pattern around the edges. She placed it in the wood-fired oven and reached for another log to stoke the fire.

"It is about time for you to head back to school," Clara Belle said as the cuckoo bird came out of the clock to announce the hour.

"Oh, don't remind me," Leah said. "Summer is ending and autumn is here."

Clara Belle smiled and said, "I like autumn." She took a sip of coffee and looked out the porch window at the aspen trees.

Clara Belle put on her skunk hat and chuckled. "The Just Family kids rode horseback to Skunk Creek School carrying their own lunch in a sock and hay in a gunnysack for the horse. They rode three miles from the ranch and the town of Tabernash in all kinds of weather between April to November."

"They went to school in the summer?" Leah asked.

"Well, they couldn't go in the winter because the snow was too deep, you see."

Leah nodded and took an apple slice from the cutting board. "Say, Rudy, when are you going to cut the hay? I'm ready to ride in the upper pastures!"

"Oh yeah? Well, now, don't go into the pastures before the hay is cut. You will trample it," Rudy reminded her. "We'll start cuttin' next week if we can get the tractor up and runnin'."

Fall meant harvest time for the hay crop. At an altitude of over nine thousand feet, there was only one cutting of mountain grass hay. The mixture of timothy grass and clover was left to grow all summer. In the fall, it was cut and put up to feed livestock throughout the winter.

"Too bad you don't use horses to harvest the hay still. It is so fun to drive a team of horses."

"Yes, working with a team of horses is rewarding, but is really hard work. We could only put up loose hay in those days, not bales of hay like today." Rudy went over to the sun porch window and pointed to the islands of wooden scaffolding that dotted the pasture. There stood several tall ramps made of pieces of timber.

"The hay would be cut, and after a couple of days it was turned to continue drying and raked into a line called 'windrows.' It would then be moved to the front of the wooden stacker called a 'beaver slide.' A double team of horses was hitched to pulley to push the hay up the scaffolding. The hay would drop off the other side and make a pile that looked like a loaf of bread." Rudy laughed. "Now the tractors come in to cut it, turn it, and the bailer spits out hay in fifty-pound bales."

Leah loved the rectangular hay bales. They were perfect jumps to jump over and perfect barrels to turn around. "Why do they say Middle Park hay is the best in the country?" Leah asked as she grabbed another apple slice.

"Well, in Colorado, a 'park' is a high mountain basin or valley, and we have three of them—North, Middle, and South. North and South Park are wide flat basins, but Middle Park is narrower. The Colorado River starts near Grand Lake and runs through Middle Park. Although the areas for hay growing are smaller, the quality of the hay is excellent." Rudy plucked the dead leaves off the geranium, then watered it. "The mowers should be here next week if the weather holds out."

The next week, the mowers did arrive and drove into the ranch like a parade to cut Rudy's hay. Praying for no rain, they worked as fast as they could to preserve the stalk's nutrition. Once the grass was cut, all that remained was short stubble. The hay bales stayed in the meadow until the stacker could finish with the neighbor's ranch and head over.

Leah and Kacy pedaled their bikes down to the ranch, enjoying the last of the rides before the snow came. Clara Belle provided sandwiches for the ranch hands on freshly baked bread. The afternoon sun was setting soon so the girls quickly ran to get the horses and headed to the upper pasture. The hay was baled and dotted the pasture.

"It is so much fun riding on the freshly cut grass. You can see every hole and every hill." Leah jumped on Dandy bareback and kicked her boots off.

"Yahoo!" She dropped her reins on Dandy's neck and hung her arms out like an airplane as he loped up the hill. Her eyes closed as the last rays of the day coated her face. She picked the reins back up, wheeled Dandy around, and headed straight for a row of hay bales. They were perfectly spaced two strides apart and she reined Dandy to jump each one.

Kacy took off in a full gallop and turn around the bales like they were barrels at the rodeo. She and Kacy crossed Pole Creek several times and winded their way through the bales to the other side. As dusk fell, they reached the far ends of the pasture at the base of Snow Mountain. The air was cooler on the upper elevation. There were few aspen leaves left there. The end of the color signaled the end of the fall season; winter was just around the corner.

The snow sputtered a bit with fall storms, then finally stuck, covering the ground with a white blanket of several feet of snow. It was fresh pristine powder with snow crystals that grabbed light and looked like glitter sparkling in the sun. Pillows of snow weighed each tree branch down, covering the evergreen pine needles with a white coat. The winter wonderland view looked like a place where Santa and his reindeer lived.

In the Yankee Doodle cabin, Leah crumbled the newspaper up in six snowball-sized wads of paper to start the fire in the unique corner fireplace. A square fort of kindling held the paper, while logs crisscrossed on top. The long wood match flared in an orange flame as Leah struck it. She lit the newspaper, and the fire roared to life as it popped and sputtered. The room filled with warmth. Leah played with her matchbox cars for a while on the stone hearth of the fireplace, then lay on the floor and colored.

The weekend was the only time Leah could get down to the Just Ranch to see the horses, when it was daylight and reasonably warm. She enjoyed school, but thoughts frequently traveled to the Ranch and the health of the horses, especially after a heavy snow. The horses seemed perfectly fine standing in three feet of snow. The temperatures frequently dropped to below zero with more than a few days of minus 20 degrees. Despite the cold days and amount of snow, the horses thrived. Rudy said it was the spring snows that were especially hard on the livestock. The snow was wet and soaked down to the skin to make an animal cold. Winter's snow was light and fluffy and despite the amount of it, the horses were happy.

Leah could tell from the frost on window that it was frigid outside. She put on a few more layers and headed out the door to the Just Ranch. She ran down the stairs of the cabin, and when her boots hit the snow, she knew she was right. *Squeak, squeak, squeak.* That was the sound of snow when the temperature falls. It was hard to breathe, and the sides of her nose stuck together, forcing her to breathe from her mouth. Steam encircled her head. Leah buried her nose in her scarf and stepped up her walk.

When she arrived at the Just Ranch, the animals seemed to go on about their business despite the cold. A small stream cut through the snow so the animals could have something to drink. It was dark against the white snow. The animals left tracks wherever they went. A beautiful ice sculpture could be seen hanging on the fence. Icicles of many shapes and sizes hung in a unique pattern on the squares of the no-climb fence. The water from the sprinkler had been left on and created the artwork.

The sheep were at the upper barn and stayed close by all winter. The snow in the corral was dirty from hay and manure. Their wool had grown to its full length and was keeping them warm for the winter. The early lambs bounced and played. Their dark bodies didn't have much wool on them. The rabbits hopped through the yard, stopping to eat bits of hay or shake the snow off their feet. Some sunned themselves next to the hutch. The goats also hung out with the sheep. Their kids ran in and out of the barn, leaping off the doorframe. The geese honked when they got too close. Only a few chickens ventured out of the chicken coup; most hunkered down and enjoyed the warmth of their coup.

The ranch house was especially cozy in the winter. The picture window gave a commanding view of the storms rolling in and out of the valley. Rudy had the fire going in the cookstove, and Clara Belle had a pot of stew on top. Leah walked down the snowmobile track to the front door.

"Come on in, honey!" Clara Belle said through the window. "Come and have something to eat." Leah closed the door quickly and pulled her boots off. She sat down at the table and smelled the stew in her bowl. It filled her with a sense of comfort. "This stew has carrots, potatoes, and onions from Rudy's garden," Clara Belle explained.

Leah took a spoonful. "It's the middle of winter and the garden is under three feet of snow. How can these vegetables come from his garden?" she asked.

"The carrots are buried in the sand and the potatoes are put in this dark barrel. There they stay protected all winter long," Clara Belle said.

"I know that feeling… I felt like I was buried in the cabin and had to get out! Leah exclaimed. "One can color for only so long until cabin fever sets in."

"Well, for fun, the Just kids played cards and board games. They had a phonograph that provided the music to practice dancing. They even skied on homemade skis. They broke through the snow to make cross-country trails," Clara Belle said.

"Oh yes, *meine Mutti* would pull us kids on skis behind a horse in the meadows." Rudy chuckled. "That was my favorite game on skis. Old Red was the best. He was a saddle horse with draft horse blood, so he was stronger and faster than our other ranch horses. He pulled us kids over little jumps we built."

"I love cross-country skiing," Leah said. "It's fun to kick and glide and sail down the hills." She motioned her arms like she was skiing and kicked her legs out. "It's hard work, but once you know how to do it, it's a blast!" With that, Leah said goodbye and headed out to the horses.

Steam billowed out of the horse's nostrils as they breathed. Long hair covered their bodies like teddy bears. Each one of them had gained extra weight to help them keep warm. Snowballs hung to the hair on the sides of their bodies like tassels. In about three and a half feet of snow in open pasture, the horses stayed in the same place. Away from any tree, barn, or shelter of any kind, there they wintered all season long. Depending on the direction the storm blew in from, they positioned their bodies with their hindquarters facing the wind, eyes partially or fully closed to avoid the ice crystals of the driving snow. In bad storms, snow would pile up on their backs, providing much-needed insulation.

Pegas was the exception. His hair did not grow much, so he knew he had to add a layer of fat to keep warm. The only long hair that grew on him was on his white spots. They looked like cotton balls glued all over his body. He was a very happy horse. His main mission in life was to conserve energy and get as fat as possible; he needed it during the winter.

To get food, the horses dug through all the snow, looking for leftover food from the summer. Their dominant front leg came up out of the snow in a striking position, then back down to the snow. Each stroke brought more snow out and closer to a few blades of grass. Finally, after the third paw through the snow, they put their heads down into the hole and pulled out a few lifeless stalks in their teeth.

Late into the winter, Rudy started feeding the horses from the hay put up the fall before. He hooked up a sled to his snowmobile, loaded it with hay, and drove it down to the pasture. They were always happy to see him. He took a moment to talk to them as they worked a treat out of his jean jacket.

"Hi, boy, how are you holding up?" Leah hugged Pegas around the neck. She took off her glove then plucked a horse cookie out of her front pocket. Pegas snapped his ears forward and snatched it out of her hands. He seemed so satisfied as he broke down the cookie in his mouth. She bent down and kissed him on his nostril.

"Now you smell like molasses!"

She took the metal bit in her hand to warm it up, then slipped the bridle on. Pegas ran his tongue under the bit a couple of times, chewing as he went. She flung the roping reins around his neck and looked for a spot to get on. The snow was deep, so every time she jumped up, the snow pulled her down.

"Let's come over here and try this, Pegas." She led him over to a frozen pile of manure and stood on top of it. Pegas waded over and sunk lower in the snow. "Perfect!" She jumped over his withers and kicked her legs the rest of the way up, then swung her leg over and sat up.

"Okay, Pegas. Let's go." Leah clucked to him and they started to head out of the horse pasture. Each step was a bit higher and slightly delayed as Pegas worked his way through the snow. He had to raise his legs so high, it was as if he was prancing. His back rolled side to side with the extra effort. Step by step, they made their way up to the barn.

"Hey, now, you made it up," Rudy said stroking a goose he was holding. She was white as snow and nibbled at his jacket, no doubt smelling the leftover horse cookies.

"I think we'll just head up to the Rowley place and back. I don't want to work him too hard when he's not used to it."

"All right. Clara Belle and I are headed into town for some supplies but should be back before dark." Rudy put the goose down and headed to the truck.

The only place to ride was on the snow-packed road, which made it really slippery for horses. On the side of the road, the snow was softer and not as slippery. But after a little while walking on the loose snow, it balled up under their hooves, making it hard for them to walk.

"Hang on, Pegas. Let me get that snow off." Leah jumped down and grabbed a stick nearby. She lifted Pegas's front leg up and stabbed the snowball until it came off in a chunk. She lifted his other leg up and flicked that one off.

"There you go, boy," Leah said, looking around. "Now, how am I going to get back on?" She pulled Pegas over to a fallen tree that was sticking out of the snowbank and lined him up as close as she could to get on. He stood farther away than she wanted. *Can I make this?* she whispered to herself. Her pants were heavy with hair and dirt from sitting on Pegas's back, and her legs ached. She took a deep squat and sprang with such force that Pegas stepped sideways in alarm. She slid down.

"Hold still, Pegas!" Leah said, out of breath. She looked around on the empty road for other ways to get on. There were none, so she moved him next to the tree again. This time, Pegas was ready when she made the leap. With extra effort, she kicked her legs as hard as possible to make it up the rest of the way.

"Pegas, I can't do that again if you get another snowball. Let's head back to the ranch."

When they made it back, Pegas was glad to be home with the other horses. He waded his way back over to them. Leah slid off and slipped the bridle off Pegas. He shook his head and started eating some leftover hay. She turned and headed up the hill to the sheep barn, wading through the deep snow. The wind was blowing and the temperature was dropping. When she got up to where the sheep were standing, she saw blood on the snow. A ewe had just given birth to twin lambs.

"Oh no! You can't have your babies out here. Rudy and Clara Belle have gone into town!" Leah assessed the lambs. They were still wet with streaks of blood and debris on them.

"There is no one here to help me," Leah said to herself. "I have to get them into the barn and into warmth as soon as possible so the coyotes don't eat them." She knew if the cold didn't get them, the coyotes would.

Leah tried to herd the ewe into the barn.

"Come on, mama, let's get you into the barn." The ewe stamped her foot, then jumped to the side. She was very skittish and would not lead or herd. Leah thought for a minute. She had seen Rudy carry newborns before, so she gathered up the twins into her arms, and headed toward the sheep barn. They made tiny *baa baa* sounds. The mama made loud, demanding *BAA BAA* sounds, not liking that Leah had them.

"Come on, mama. Come with your lambs into the barn and out of the cold." As she had hoped, the mama followed along behind her, not wanting to leave the lambs. It was hard to walk through the snow, but Leah made it to the sheep barn. She walked through the barn door along with the mama and another pregnant ewe.

"Wait, no. You can't come in." The ewe stamped her foot and stayed next to the mama's side, determined not to leave. Leah tried to push her out of the barn, but she quickly circled back. Did the other ewe want to steal the babies away?

"For now, you'll stay. I have to take care of the lambs." Leah knew she had no time to waste, so she let all four of them stay in the barn. There was a small pen with straw in it. She opened the gate with her foot, and laid the lambs down in the straw. A heat lamp hung over the stall. Leah turned it on. A red glow lit the room. She got some fresh hay from the hayloft and put it around the lambs. She watched them through the slats of the fence as the mama cleaned them. They shivered, but were alert and seemed happy to be in the barn. Their beautiful eyes explored the new world that they had been born into. She kept watch over them for about an hour before she heard a truck rumble up the driveway.

Leah ran out of the barn. She grabbed some snow to "wash" the blood off her coat as she made her way over to the truck.

"Rudy!" she shouted. "A ewe just delivered twin lambs in the snow. I moved them to the barn." Rudy closed the truck door and quickly followed Leah over to the barn. Leah told him everything she had done, and when he saw for himself he said, "You did good. The ewe and lambs needed help, and you gave it to them. Thank you."

"But why did this other ewe insist on coming with us?" Leah asked, still bothered that she was in the barn.

"Oh, they do that sometimes when they themselves are close to giving birth. It was right to not fight her and to let her come along. She needed the comfortable barn too."

After giving a hug to Rudy and Clara Belle, Leah started the long walk home. This time, she was not cold at all but filled with pride for doing the right thing for the ewe and her precious babies.

The next day, Leah's dad pulled up to the cabin in the "Green Streak." The 1965 Chevy Suburban was used for everything needed around the camp. including maintenance, housekeeping. and hauling guests. It was big and boxy and looked like a cartoon vehicle.

"Come on, Leah. It's time to go get the Christmas tree. There is a storm coming and we need to get back before the snow falls." He drove deeper into the woods of the ranch. Finally, the road narrowed with the snowbanks, which prevented her dad from driving any further. There was no way to turn around, and it worried Leah that they might get stuck in the remote location, especially if the snow hit before they finished.

"Let's go from here on foot to find the perfect tree." Her dad opened the back doors and grabbed the saw. The snow was deep as they waded out into the forest. There was a group of spruce trees mixed in with a grove of aspen and pine. Rabbit tracks dotted the snow, along with smaller dots in a more parallel pattern. Suddenly, the snow moved. Leah gasped. "Look!" She pointed to an open patch. There on top of the snow ran a snow minx. Its long, thin body glided over the powder. It was all white except for its brown eyes and nose. There was a tiny brown tip on its tail.

"Wow, how lucky we are to see something so rare and beautiful!" Leah's dad said. She watched it run across the snow in a random way as if greeting its strange visitors. It ducked under some branches and went out of sight.

Leah scanned the woods for more of a sign of the minx, but then her eye settled on something more interesting. Within the mounds of white, Leah saw it: the perfect Christmas tree. It was standing alone next to the grove with a pristine shape. It was a little tall, but Leah knew her dad could trim it.

"Dad, look! I found it! Our Christmas tree!"

"That is a perfect Christmas tree, but we don't want that one," he said.

"But why not?" Leah protested.

"We want to try to find a tree that is being crowded out, one that won't have a chance to grow well or one that is crowding other trees out." They walked deep into the grove of spruce trees and found one that fit that description.

"It is not perfect, but perfect for us," he admitted. The tree had a pretty side, but on the back there was a hole where the branches didn't grow. "Let's get this back. I'm sure we can trim it up nicely." Leah's dad scooped the snow out from the bottom of the tree and sawed back and forth until, *crack*, the trunk gave way and the tree fell over with a *whoosh*.

"Grab those branches and let's drag the tree back to the truck." Walking through the deep snow was hard enough, but dragging a tree made it even harder. The weight of the tree sunk down on the top layer of the snow and left a track like a broom. Leah held on tight to the car handle as her dad backed down the road. It seemed to be forever before there was a spot to turn around.

Once home, they unloaded the tree and got it set up in the stand. It was crooked, and the hole on the backside was a little more obvious than they had expected. When it came time to decorate, her mom and Kacy were less than enthusiastic about the tree, but everyone knew why it was chosen and felt good about their decision. Candy canes and ornaments were hung from the tree. Tinsel made it sparkle, and red balls gave it balance.

Her father built a fire with logs stored on the porch. Her mother made hot chocolate and dressed the chocolate cake with candy canes. Leah snuggled up in her pajamas and thought of the horses in their winter coats. The fire popped. Huge snowflakes floated down from the gray sky. It would be a while until spring arrived, and the robins made their way back to the Just Ranch.

Colorado Chocolate Cake

Ingredients:

3 cups all-purpose flour

2 cups white sugar

1 teaspoon salt

2 teaspoons baking soda

1/2 cup unsweetened cocoa powder

3/4 cup vegetable oil

2 tablespoons distilled white vinegar

2 teaspoons vanilla extract

2 cups cold water

Directions:

1. Sift flour, sugar, salt, soda, and cocoa together, and then pour into a 9 x 13 inch ungreased cake pan.
2. Make three wells. Pour oil into one well, vinegar into second, and vanilla into third well. Pour cold water over all, and stir well with fork.
3. Bake at 350 degrees Fahrenheit for 30 to 40 minutes, or until tooth pick inserted comes out clean.
4. Decorate with candy canes on each piece, frost with chocolate frosting or eat plain.

Rudy and Clara Belle Just, with Collie and Happy.

Patrice and Cindy with Charlie the goat.

Patrice on Spice and Cindy on Penny with the valley view before Pole Creek Golf Course was built. Sheep are grazing in the pasture with the backdrop of the Continental Divide.

Rudy's horse Buck.

A ewe at the sheep barns with a black bunny behind her.

A lamb sunning himself in front of the horse barn.

One of the many rabbits that lived at the Just Ranch

Rudy with his skis around age 12.

Clara Belle in her fringe chaps as a cowgirl in Western
Colorado before she met and married Rudy.

Patrice on Pegas with Hermie the squirrel in front of her home,
Yankee Doodle Cabin.

In the sheep pasture below the ranch house, Patrice on Pegas getting
a cold drink from Pole Creek with Cindy leading Brandy.

Rudy and Clara Belle Just. She is holding a basket made by a Cherokee Indian visitor
from willow branches similar to those that grow on the banks of Pole Creek.

For more photos, please visit TalesofaYoungRider.com.

ABOUT THE ILLUSTRATOR

Andie has been doing digital art for as long as she can remember. She feels the colors and shapes offer the best way to convey the story. Andie's interests include soccer, art, cooking, and flying. She lives in Northern California with her family and dog, Mei.

About the Author

Having grown up at YMCA of the Rockies, Snow Mountain Ranch, Patrice Engle Spyrka has firsthand knowledge of the rich history and many adventures of pioneer life in Colorado. Mountains, horses, and cross-country skiing are in her blood, as is an acute fear of bears!

She graduated from Colorado State University and owned a historic ranch in Elbert. She now lives in Northern California with her husband, two daughters, and dog, Alvin.

Find out more about Patrice Engle Spyrka by visiting TalesofaYoungRider.com, and on social media @TalesofaYoungRider.

CPSIA information can be obtained
at www.ICGtesting.com
Printed in the USA
BVHW022324130621
609330BV00002B/4